PAYBACK TIME!

The point man was so close I couldn't risk a whisper. He stopped just steps beyond us. I could see his trigger finger tense as he sniffed the air. Then he eased his trigger grip and waved the others forward. It was killing time. The wild scream from my oscillating weapon riveted full-auto lead into the forward figures. Cassidy's M16 hammered rapid-fire bursts. The pelting lead bit into their bodies, jerking them like puppets on a string . . .

"As real and shocking as an M16 on full auto. COMMAND AND CONTROL is chock-full of the details that authenticate Jim Mitchell as a true combat veteran."

—Mark Berent, author of
ROLLING THUNDER

COMMAND AND CONTROL

PAYBACK MISSION

by
JAMES D. MITCHELL

BERKLEY BOOKS, NEW YORK

COMMAND AND CONTROL: PAYBACK MISSION

A Berkley Book / published by arrangement with
the author

PRINTING HISTORY
Berkley edition / August 1990

ISBN: 0-425-12216-6

A BERKLEY BOOK® TM 757,375
Berkley Books are published by The Berkley Publishing Group,
200 Madison Avenue, New York, New York 10016.
The name ''BERKLEY'' and the ''B'' logo
are trademarks belonging to Berkley Publishing Corporation.

DEDICATION
This book is dedicated to my fallen Special
Forces comrades who gave their lives
defending freedom in Southeast Asia; and
to the handful of United States Marines I
had the brief privilege of serving with on
Hill 950, 1968.

ACKNOWLEDGMENTS
Grateful appreciation is conveyed to the
combined membership of the Trinity Arts
Writers Association, Jim Morris, Amelia
Mitchell, and Syble Mitchell, whose
collective and thoughtful critique helped
shape this story. Additional thanks to my
agent, Peter Miller, of NYC.

Author's note: Readers' comments about this story and other
Command and Control novels are appreciated. Comments may
be addressed to: James D. Mitchell
P.O. Box 1885 Hurst, TX 76053.

Chapter 1

A distant clatter of monsoon thunder rumbled through the open window of my hospital room. From my bed I saw the rush of dark clouds blow in from the west, whipping Old Glory and the Vietnamese colors wildly about the flagpoles. The damp smell of impending rain swirled through the air. A rhythmic pinging echoed as the winds thrashed the metal lanyard trolleys against the steel poles.

It could have been the noise that woke me, but it was more likely my restless recon habit of always waking at first light.

First light. It stabbed slowly through the jungle canopy, like a mosquito probing its snout through my shirt to penetrate the flesh, then suck my blood.

First light was Chuck, the NVA, probing and weaving through the dim jungle shadows of Laos, thirsty for more American blood.

I raised myself slowly, feeling the taut grip of bandages surrounding my chest. Easing my legs off the side of the bed, I stood and glanced at the wall calendar. The calendar pictured a shapely Vietnamese girl with a caption that read, ''September is near end of monsoon season for my Vietnam. Soon come dry season toward late October.''

The date was September 25, 1969. They'd removed my IV five days ago. Today, I was looking forward to being released and returning to base camp CCN, and my team.

I'd been in 'Nam almost eleven months, here in the 95th medevac hospital eight days. And now, after fourteen missions I could no longer boast that I'd come through a Special Forces tour here without a scratch.

I wasn't complaining. It could have been a lot worse. Fortunately, the fallen teak tree I had taken cover behind during that clusterfuck firefight had absorbed most of the impact from the B-40 rocket explosion.

I had scratches all right, not to mention cuts and bruises. My eyes had recovered from the temporary blindness, but my chest and shoulders looked like they'd caught fire and somebody had put it out with a track shoe. Even now, I felt an itching beneath the bandages like there were still some shattered tree splinters in me.

Arnold Binkowski, my new Yankee assistant team leader, had been the hero that afternoon when the defecation hit the cooling apparatus and my lights went out.

Recon Team Texas, two Americans and four Montagnards, was knee-deep in a supersonic hardball firefight and struggling to get to our exfil LZ with an NVA prisoner.

With maximized guts and a little displaced luck of the Polish, Ski led the team and broke contact. He carried my six-foot, two-hundred-pound limp body through three hundred meters of thick jungle to the exfil LZ.

I'd regained consciousness by the time we finally got to the LZ, but then, Chuck hit us hard again. During the firefight, our prisoner tried to strangle Ski. I killed that bald NVA shanker scab with a knife.

I leaned forward and stretched, touching my toes to determine if I was still experiencing any pain. None.

I knew it would be a while before I got back to a three-hundred-pound bench press. But at least I wouldn't be benching with one arm, or trying to run on one leg.

Bobby Rodriguez, my Marine roommate, hadn't been as lucky. He'd lost his left leg during a VC assault on Hill 950 a week before.

I hadn't noticed him stir before his sleepy voice broke into my thoughts. "Shit, Yancy! I know you're getting outa here today, man, but it looks like you're starting PT already! You snake eaters must like pain or something." He grinned, pushing himself up in bed and reaching for a cigarette.

I glanced at the flat area of bed sheet below his left hip. They'd had to cut high into Bobby's upper leg to save his life. I walked around his bed and struck a match for him.

"Well," I said, pulling the flame away and blowing it out with a quick breath. "I've gotta try and stay in shape, Rod. I mean, with you heading back Stateside soon, one of us has got to stay here and win this fuckin' war."

He looked down, blowing the first draw of smoke over the flat spot of sheet. "Yeah, well good luck winning this war, Brett. Frankly, I tend to agree with your fiancée, Tracy. This is a fuckin' commercial war, man, and nobody in a position to end it wants to. There're too many people at home, and here, getting rich on this war, man!"

Right from the first day together, over a week ago now, Bobby Rodriguez and I had been friends. No pretense, no ingratiating bullshit, and no shoulder crying about our wounds. The tougher ground was being hoed by Bobby. I was recovering from my wounds, but his left leg was lying on some shit stench patch of jungle north of Khe Sanh and there wasn't any goddamn recovering from that.

I tossed the match into the ashtray, then turned toward the window and closed it. Looking back at him, I said, "I'm heading down to the latrine to shave and make a deposit for Uncle Ho Chi Minh's funeral fund. You need a bedpan, Rod?"

He looked out toward the stormy sky, then glanced back at me with a forced smile. "No thanks, man . . ." His voice rose with a dramatized enthusiastic tone. "They're takin' me down to X ray first thing this morning. I think I'll stay here and shine my boot while I'm waiting!" He winked.

I tried to smile back but could feel only about half of it. Even though my smile wasn't working, I couldn't conceal the admiration in my eyes. Feeling my smile start to fade, I turned and spoke while walking out the door. "Yeah, some guys will do anything to get out of shining a boot. Be right back, Rod. I'll see if I can commandeer us some nachos for breakfast."

He laughed. "Okay, Brett. Dream on! Just tell 'em to beam us up some *cervesa* while you're in fantasy-land, buddy."

A taste for nachos, tacos, and good Tex-Mex food in general was just one of the things Bobby and I had in common. He was from San Antonio and I was from Cowtown—Fort Worth. We figured that made us second cousins, blood brothers, and country comrades all rolled into one.

The first couple of days together we talked about wine, women, song, and so on. But after that the subject turned to the war. He told me about the VC assault that cost him his leg. He said they had seen the VC massing in the saddle between Hill 950 and Hill 1015 long before the attack. Even though the sky was clear and perfect for air support, Lieutenant Madigan, the hill commander, wouldn't call for it.

Rod said he'd overheard the gunny recommend calling for napalm, but the lieutenant grew enraged, screaming, "Goddammit, Sergeant, we'll hold this fucking hill without them prima-donna sky jockeys gettin' all the credit! Bring it on, Charlie. Bring it fuckin' on!"

Charlie brought it on, all right. Eleven good lives and one leg later, Madigan still had his hill and his pride. The gunny, Sergeant Jackson, was killed in the first wave.

I told Rod about losing my One-One, assistant team leader, William Washington, in Laos. And how I'd been able to identify the escaping sniper by his bald head. What I hadn't told Bobby was that my last mission, the one that put me here, was preplanned by me to find and slay the hairless NVA bastard I called Baldy.

Moments later I nearly gagged as I walked into the heavy odor of Pine Sol disinfectant in the latrine. I coughed loudly.

A black Marine with a semper-fi patch on his pajamas stood near a sink. He grinned into the mirror at me. "Yeah, I know what you mean, man. This place smells like somebody's been shittin' invisible Christmas trees in here!"

I laughed, then stood in front of a urinal with a hand-painted likeness of Ho Chi Minh. The face was painted in such a way that the lower lip of the urinal formed his open mouth.

Standing there, my thoughts focused on Hill 950. Bobby had told me a lot about the hill they called Firebase Zulu. He'd been there five months when he was hit. He said they had been taking everything from rocket and mortar assaults to suicide attacks for the past several months. It was apparent the VC wanted to make the hill too costly for the Marines to stay there. But the question that hammered at me was, why in the hell is Charlie expending so much effort on a hill with little or no strategic value? Perhaps Bobby Rodriguez knew why, but if so, he hadn't revealed the reason to me.

As I returned from the latrine, my eyes caught sight of the large white-cloaked figure of Lieutenant Tritt lumbering into the nurses' station with a copy of *Sports Illustrated*.

Tritt was an abrupt type of woman with shoulders any halfback would be proud of. She was from Green Bay, Wisconsin. I got the impression she'd prefer to be playing for the Packers.

She jammed IV needles into me like they were football air needles and the ref was in a hurry to get the ball back. Her appearance and attitude were a far cry from the more shapely and personable Helen Goodwin, who shared morning duty with her.

As I approached the station she looked up and spoke in her usual matter-of-fact voice. "Morning, Sergeant Yancy."

I glanced at the wall clock above her, then leaned against the bar type railing between us. "Good morning, *Trung-'uy*. Where's Helen? She's usually here by now."

Tritt looked up from her magazine like I'd interrupted the Super Bowl. "Sergeant Yancy, I've told you countless times not to call me *trung-'uy*. *Trung-'uy* is Vietnamese for 'lieutenant,' and I'm not in the Vietnamese Army. I'm in the U.S. Army . . . like you."

I restrained the urge to tell her that we were not in the same army—only the name was coincidental.

Her massive bosom expanded as she drew in another breath and placed her hands on her hips. "Helen, rather, Lieutenant Goodwin, is in the officers' mess having breakfast with that journalist friend of yours, Tracy Gibbs."

Smiling to myself, I thought, Tracy's probably winding up one more interview before she heads back Stateside tomorrow.

Tritt turned and reached for a thermometer. "I might as well take your temperature while you're here. It'll save me a trip down to your room."

"Roger. Whatever it takes to save you some steps, *Trung*, uh, Lieutenant. This will be my last one. I'm checking out of here today. I won't be seeing you any—"

She butted in. "You better knock on wood, Yancy!" She paused to jam the glass tube into my mouth.

Placing both hands flat on the desktop, she looked up from the fluorescent glow of the desk lamps with a tilt of her head. Her mood seemed to change.

Her voice sounded pleaful. "For the life of me, I can't understand why you want to stay in Vietnam. They wanted to send you home. For God's sake, Brett, you've been here over ten months now, and darn near got your posterior blown off. But no, it appears you want to try and use up your last life!"

Her voice softened as she leaned over to pull the thermometer from my mouth. She kept her gaze on me without bothering to check the thermometer. "Look, Brett, I know you and I aren't going to be pen pals when you leave here; we've had our differences. But I'm in the caring business, and I care about what happens to you.

Don't you understand? You've done your share here.
Tracy loves you. Why don't you go home like she wants
you to? Get married, get a mortgage—have some kids!''

Her last soft words floated over me like a net.

I stood slowly away from the counter and inspected
the imploring dark eyes before me. I'd never seen her
look so sincere. I'd heard similar versions of the same
pitch from Tracy, Helen, and even Colonel Kahn, my
commander. But the words coming from Tritt rippled
through me like the opening jerk of a parachute.

She was being sincere. She deserved a straight answer.
Leaning forward, I placed my elbows on the wooden railing.

I tried to assemble words in a way she'd understand.
''During my last year in high school our football team
went to state. We played our best and still lost the game.
By the middle of the fourth quarter, eight of my team-
mates had been sidelined with injuries. I played the last
quarter with what I found out later was a cracked rib.''

I paused and turned my head to peer at the jagged
ribbon of morning light reflecting off the polished hallway. ''You know about me losing my partner, Will
Washington, a few weeks back. Well, I loved Will. I
loved him like my own brother. So you see, I'm not
leaving this goddamn game till the final whistle blows.
RT Texas was Will's team, and I'm pressing on the same
way I know he would.''

I stood away from the counter and tried to smile. ''I
don't expect you or anyone else to understand the way I
feel, but I do thank you for your concern . . .'' I paused,
then winked. ''By the way, Bobby and I could sure use
some nachos and beer for breakfast.''

She ignored my attempted wit and withdrew a file from
a stack on the desk. She flipped the folder open and re-

turned to her authoritative voice. "Okay, Brett Yancy, if you insist on going back to war, hear this: Dr. Ostman has cleared you for duty—light duty! That means no lifting, no jumping, no bending, no reaching . . ."

Her voice trailed off as she looked up with a smirk. "Not going to be much of a war for you with these restrictions. Can you type?" She smirked.

I cracked a half smile. Ultimately, Colonel Kahn would decide how much I could handle, not this candy-assed medical bureaucracy. Nodding toward the thermometer in her hand, I said, "Ninety-eight point five," then started back to the ward. Turning, I gave her a final wave and said, "Thanks for the info, *Trung-'uy, chao-ong.*"

Chapter 2

When I entered my room an orderly was taking Bobby out on a gurney. He grinned as they wheeled him past me. "Be back later, Yancy. This dude is going to take some flicks of me for X-ray quarterly. I may be next month's centerfold."

I walked to the window and gazed out at the rainy courtyard. My thoughts drifted to Tracy Gibbs. We'd met on a flight to Thailand two days after I'd lost William Washington. Colonel Kahn had directed me to take a leave to get my head back together.

The leave may have helped my head, but it was Tracy who put the first stitches in my heart. She was the greatest thing since napalm and thirty-round magazines. Tracy was a tall, good-looking blond assemblage of wit, sensuality, and intelligence. She had a non-neon type of charm and true-grit expression that damn near put her in the too-good-to-be-true category.

She had been in 'Nam for the past ten months doing human-interest stories for *Personality Magazine*. When our trails crossed, we were both en route to a holiday in Thailand.

I smiled, remembering a quote from Casanova, "The

essence of womanhood is the ability to inspire love and arousal in men.'' Maybe some of that was true. In the four days we'd spent together, she almost ''inspired'' me into blissful exhaustion.

But with Tracy the inspiration sparked something more in me: a genuine belief in the long-term possibility of happiness with one splendid woman.

After returning from Thailand, Tracy went on to Saigon to do an interview with General Creighton Abrams and I went back to war. When she heard I was hit she dropped everything and flew directly to Da Nang. I remembered waking after surgery and sensing her familiar fragrance and the warmth of her hand caressing mine.

A day later, right before falling asleep, I asked her to marry me. When I woke up Tracy was gone, but there was a note tucked under my hospital ID band. It read:

Dear Brett:

  I've gone to make some calls. You may not remember asking me to marry you, but if you do, the answer is yes—anytime, anyplace. However, it's common for men to say some strange things coming out of anesthesia. It would never hold up in a court of law! (Ha, ha, just kidding.) We'll both be going back to the States soon—you can ask me again then and the answer will be the same. I'll be back in one hour.

                                                    Love, Tracer

Tracy Gibbs had tracked into my life with the glow and velocity of a tracer round headed straight for my heart. And now, Tracer, as I nicknamed her, was as much a part of my life as Will Washington.

My eyes caught a reflective glimpse off the window-pane. Two stout, beret-clad figures moved through the doorway. I turned and saw the residue of rain glistening and dripping off the ponchos of Colonel Ivan Kahn and Arnold Binkowski.

Ski was beaming from ear to ear. True to his impet-uous nature, he hurried toward me ahead of Colonel Kahn. "Mo'ning Sahgeant Yancy."

Ski should have called attention, but we both knew the colonel wasn't big on protocol. Nonetheless, I snapped a sharp salute to Colonel Kahn. I was glad they'd caught me standing. For the past week, during their visits, I'd always been lying in bed. Now, I hoped my appearance carried the positive message that I was ready to get back to my team—back to work.

Ivan Kahn returned my salute, smiled broadly, and extended his hand. "Good morning, Brett. You look good. How you feeling?"

I smiled, shaking his hand firmly. "Strong as five acres of garlic, sir. I'm ready to get back to earning my pay."

I glanced up at Ski. His blond-topped six-foot three-inch mesomorphic frame put him about two inches taller than me. He was wearing a bright new pair of E-5 chev-rons on his fatigue shirt. I shook his hand, saying, "Is that somebody else's shirt or have you been promoted, partner?"

Binkowski's voice rose proudly. "Yeah . . . I mean, roger that. Colonel Kahn promoted me to sahgeant yes-terday."

Ski's accent made the absence of an "R" in sergeant sound like it was a foreign promotion. I grinned and

mimicked him. "Sahgeant, is that something like a sergeant?"

His smile broadened. He was used to being teased
about his Boston brogue. "Roger that, Brett. One and
the same."

"Congratulations, buddy. You deserve it." I winked.
"And by the way, thanks for pulling my ass outa the
wringer out there. I'd say for a man on his first combat
mission you did damn good."

He glanced down shyly, then looked up with a lopsided
grin. "Thanks, Brett. But, the truth is, I was scared shit-
less. I must've been on automatic pilot or something.
You may not remember too much about those last minutes before we got to the chopper. You were delirious, I
thought you were dying, partner."

His eyes saddened for a moment. "Anyhow, right in
the middle of the mud and the blood and the bullets, our
prisoner tried to strangle me. You must have sensed it
somehow, because during the struggle I felt his grip on
my neck go slack. When I looked back, Baldy was lying
face-up with your knife jammed in his gut. He jerked
and quivered for a few seconds, then went limp. When I
glanced at you, you smiled, then passed out again. There
was nothing I could do right then, Brett. We had fucking
NVA all over us."

Ski blinked, then looked away and spoke softly. "Like
I said, you may not remember any of that."

I remembered the moment all right. When my blade
rammed hilt-deep into his gut, the warm greasy flow of
his death blood over my fingers felt good—damn good.

Colonel Kahn darted a sharp gaze at Ski. "Baldy? Did
I hear you call him Baldy?"

Ski glanced at me before answering Colonel Kahn.
"Yes, sir. He was as clean shaven as a cue ball."

Ivan Kahn turned to me with questioning eyes. "So that's how you were able to identify him as Sergeant Washington's assassin? By his bald head?"

I nodded. "Roger, sir. He was sniping from a tree. He hit Will with two rounds square in the back. As Will fell I fired a burst up into the tree. I didn't hit him, but it had to have knocked his dick string loose because he crashed through the limbs and hung by a lower branch. Then he dropped to the ground and hobbled into the bush. When he fell through the tree he must have lost his pith helmet. The last thing I saw was his shiny head disappearing into the jungle."

My mind churned back to the bitter moments when I had to make a split-second decision: whether to pursue the bastard or get to Will and try and save him. I ran to Will's trembling body and frantically tried to stop the bleeding, but he died in my arms a few moments later. His final soft message to his wife still rang quietly in my mind. "Tell Chunky I'm going 'cross the river, man. I'll see her and the kids over there. Might even see you there someday, boss."

The body recovery mission we'd conducted that hot Asian morning had been a tragic trade—the recovery of three down and dead helicopter crewmen for Will's life.

When Chuck ambushed us on the LZ, Will was hit hard, but he kept returning fire to cover the team. He nailed four NVA assaulting him at point-blank range, then hurled a well-placed grenade into a B-40 rocket team near him.

Will might have lived if Baldy's sniper rounds hadn't ripped through his back. William Washington saved us that fateful morning—he saved the mission and gave up his life for the recovery of three American warriors.

I loved Will. My loneliest regret was that I waited until

his dying moments to tell him. Perhaps he knew it without words, but I'd never forgive myself for letting my displaced sense of manhood prevent me from saying it sooner.

Colonel Kahn's grip on my shoulder brought my blurred eyes up to his. "Brett, I know it's tough on you reliving that memory, but I've got to ask you something."

"Have you seen any other bald, clean-shaven NVA on any of your operations in Laos?"

I felt my jaw tighten. "Negative, sir. Not one."

I was puzzled by the urgency in his voice. He went on to explain that recent intel reports alluded to the possibility of some key NVA officers playing a Jekyll and Hyde role. By shaving their heads they could put on orange robes and move freely throughout the area with the local Buddhist monks. It was well known that the monks sympathized with and supported the Communists. Upon successful infiltration of our areas, the bastards could then conduct dead-letter drops, observe and map various camp defenses, and even plan and lead night sapper attacks.

Right now, the intel speculation was unconfirmed, but if it turned out to be true, it could be the most ingenious method of enemy infiltration since the invention of the Trojan Horse.

"Damn! I almost forgot, Brett. I brought your fatigues and boots. They're in a rucksack, out in the jeep. Be right back." Ski hurried out the door.

I reached for an envelope on my nightstand and handed it to Colonel Kahn. "Sir, this is my recommendation for an award for Binkowski. Silver Star. I wouldn't be standing here now if it weren't for that big Yankee."

He smiled, stashed the envelope under his poncho, then removed his wet beret and began wringing the water out while holding it over a wastebasket. "I'm sure President Kennedy was paying us the ultimate compliment when he awarded the green beret to Special Forces, but I wish they'd made it a little more waterproof."

Straightening his beret, he looked back at me, then carefully repositioned it over his thick gray hair. "There won't be any problem on your award recommendation, Brett. Binkowski did a damn fine job out there. And, speaking of awards, you'll be pleased to know that Will Washington's Medal of Honor has been approved. They'll be having a special presentation ceremony at Fort Bragg in November, and since you'll be back there by then, I sort of volunteered you to make the presentation to his wife."

I knew it hadn't been easy for Colonel Kahn to get the award approved. For weeks the MACV Saigon bureaucrats had tried to downgrade and sidestep the award. But my commander didn't back down. At the risk of biting the hands that wrote his efficiency report, he went above their heads to the Pentagon. Now, at last, it was approved.

"Thank you, sir . . . And yes, sir, it will be a privilege to present Will's award to his family."

Chapter 3

Colonel Kahn reached under his poncho and withdrew a cigarette. He spoke while lighting it. "I'm sending Sergeant Binkowski down to One-Zero school at Long Thanh. They have a class beginning next Monday."

The news didn't surprise me. It was standard procedure to send an assistant team leader, a One-One, to recon team-leader school as soon as possible after he was assigned to a team.

One-Zero school was a three-week crash course in everything related to Special Forces combat reconnaissance operations. I'd attended it one month after coming into RT Texas. The course culminated with a four-day live fire mission into an area selected as high-volume enemy activity—you were expected to make hostile contact. If you came back alive, you got a hearty handshake, a smile, and a graduation certificate.

I felt confident the school would be a cakewalk for Ski. He was in excellent shape and I'd already given him several weeks of related training prior to launching on the last mission.

If a picture is worth a thousand words, one combat operation into Laos had an equally proportionate benefit compared to classroom hours at recon school. The VC and the NVA weren't going to throw anything at Arnold Binkowski he hadn't already proven that he could handle.

But the news told me something else—RT Texas would now be on stand-down, no missions, until Ski returned from school. That wouldn't bother the Yards any. It'd give them a couple of weeks' leave. But it did bother me. I'd been shit at and hit hard by the NVA during this last mission, and I was eager to get back into the arena. Not that I had suicidal tendencies; I just equated it with having a malfunction on a parachute jump—either you let fear get a grip on you and quit, or you grab another chute and go up and make another jump right away.

Colonel Kahn took a long draw on his cigarette and walked slowly over to the rain-pelted window. I sensed he had something else to say by the way he blew his smoke against the glass. A fog of warm breath condensed on the glass, disappearing as he spoke.

"Brett, I talked with Doc Ostman yesterday concerning your physical condition. He's put you on light duty, and I really don't want to butt heads with him on this one." He turned with a raised eyebrow. "The hospital staff gave me a lot of flak about my request to let you stay in 'Nam.

"Of course you know, with Binkowski down at One-Zero school, the team will be on stand-down for three weeks."

I hung on his words hoping he wasn't going to ask me if I could type. "Roger, sir. Understand."

"Now, Sergeant-Major Twitty could use some help up in the admin shop." He glanced at me with a sly grin to let me know he was kidding.

Twitty was a first-rate asshole. The colonel knew I'd

sooner slide down a razor blade into a tub of alcohol than work for that pencil-pushing sergeant-major.

His next words carried a note of optimism. "What I've got in mind is having you work a radio-relay slot on a hill up north. The man I have up there now, Sergeant Jacob Ray, is long overdue to rotate back. I need someone to replace him that knows and understands our operations.

"I'm inserting two teams into DMZ targets on October seventh. While they're in the lion's mouth they'll need a guardian angel. You'd be up there about a month and that would put you ready to go home. How do you feel about that?"

I knew Colonel Kahn was thin on personnel. He needed me in that slot or he wouldn't have proposed it. The answer was yes. The only part I didn't like about it was that it meant I'd run my last mission with RT Texas. The last mission with a team that Will and I had molded into one of the best at CCN. We'd won the unwavering allegiance and trust of our Montagnards, and we'd kicked ass all up and down Uncle Ho's hemorrhoid trail—sometimes got our ass kicked. Now, I felt like a dad who'd suddenly been told he had to give up his kids for adoption. I didn't like leaving them and I didn't like having to entrust their lives to someone else's judgment.

Tuong, Phan, Lok, and Rham were still teenagers by American definition, but those brave little hard chargers had fought and sweated through fourteen frying pan-to-fire missions with me and Will and that put us about as close as six people can get.

Colonel Kahn walked to the far side of Bobby's bed, crushed his cigarette into the ashtray, and looked over at me—waiting.

I looked back at the five-and-a-half-foot giant stature

of a man I respected. "Roger, sir. I know how critical radio-relay can be. It saved my ass once. Put me in, Coach."

I grinned and added, "Of course, it's going to be a real heartbreaker to Sergeant-Major Twitty, not having me around, but I imagine he'll get over it in ten or fifteen seconds. What's my destination?"

"Hill Nine-fifty. The Marines call it Firebase Zulu. It's located about seven klicks north of Khe Sanh."

His words echoed through me like the distant tolling of a bell. My eyes involuntarily glanced down at Bobby Rodriguez's bed.

"There's about twenty Marines holding down a tough patch of real estate up there. For some unknown reason the VC are turning that hill into a geographical pissing contest. The Marines pulled out of Khe Sanh over a year ago now, but I guess that wasn't good enough for Charlie. I don't know the hill commander's name right now—"

"Madigan, sir. Lieutenant Madigan!" A frown gripped my face.

The colonel's eyes narrowed. "How did you—?"

"Here you are, Brett. Sorry I took so long, but I ran into this nurse in the hall, and she couldn't resist me." Ski grinned as he set my ruck on the bed, saying, "I guess there's just something about a man in uniform."

I noticed the rucksack was dry. Then, I noticed that Ski noticed I noticed. Somehow, I knew he was going to explain it all without an invitation. Arnold was a competent soldier, but at times he was like a frustrated rocket scientist who wanted to tell the world how we got to the moon and back, in detail. I listened with restrained patience.

"You're probably wondering why your ruck is dry.

The reason is because I tucked it up under my poncho so your fatigues wouldn't get wet. That's probably what got the nurse's attention. I think she thought I was pregnant. Anyhow, your Beretta is in there too." He pointed to my ruck. "Oh, and here's your watch," he said, pulling it from under his poncho.

Glancing at his watch, Colonel Kahn said, "Brett, we've got to get headed on over to Navy base. They don't know it yet, but I'm about to commandeer an air-conditioner from them for our dispensary." He looked up at Ski. "If they give me any trouble, I'll have Sergeant Binkowski come down on them with all fours."

"Roger, sir." I shifted my eyes to Ski. "Sergeant Binkowski! That's got kind of a nice ring to it. Don't you think, partner?"

Ski grinned, looking down at his new stripes, "Yeah, it does. Almost poetic."

I turned and saluted Colonel Kahn.

He spoke while returning my salute. "We'll be coming back here in a couple of hours to get you, Brett. That'll give you time to get dressed and say your good-byes."

Good-byes. The word snapped in my mind like a dry twig. I'd forgotten about Tracy. She was leaving for the States in the morning and we'd planned on spending our last night together in Da Nang. And I'd forgotten to ask Colonel Kahn if I could take a day leave and stay in town tonight.

I cleared my throat. "Ah . . . sir . . . You met my fiancée the other day while you were here. Tracy Gibbs. Well, she's leaving to go back to New York in the morning, and I was—"

"Say no more, Yancy. We'll see you back at camp in the morning. Just keep a sharp eye out. Ever since Ho

Chi Minh's death there's been a sharp increase in urban VC activity.''

As he turned to walk away he looked back and grinned, "And remember, Brett, you're on light duty!"

Ski smirked while shaking my hand. "Yeah, that's right, light duty . . ." His words trailed behind him as he turned and followed the colonel down the hall, "No bending, no heavy lifting. Have a good night, partner."

A roar of monsoon thunder muffled his fading laughter.

I watched them disappear down the hall, then walked back into my room. I put on my fatigue pants and boots, then placed the Beretta and a full magazine on the bed. I slipped into my shoulder holster and picked up my pistol. Holding it in my open palm I noticed dark blotches of crusted blood on the grips—my blood. I jammed the magazine into the well and flipped the safety on.

Scratching the blood off the grips with my fingernail, I thought back to the last mission. The NVA hit us like a swarm of piranhas on a hamhock. Their lead was already doing a job chewing up the teak tree in front of us when they fired a B-40 rocket into it. During the insane seconds right before my lights went out, I oddly remembered the words of an instructor at Fort Bragg. He was holding a Soviet-made B-40 up in front of our class. "Gents, this son of a bitch is awesome. It can penetrate ninety-two inches of sandbagged fortification at a range of one hundred meters."

I slipped the Beretta into my shoulder holster and muttered to myself, "Awesome isn't the word for it—more like awe shit!"

"Are you talking to yourself, Brett Yancy?"

Tracy's words were followed by a quick kiss on the ear.

I turned and smiled into her emerald eyes, then looked her over. She wore tailored military fatigues and tan sandals. Above the right pocket was a name tag I'd had made for her, "Tracer." I slipped my hand around the nape of her neck and felt the smoothness of her blond hair float though my fingers.

"Talking to myself . . . ? Well, yes, I sometimes do that when no one's looking or slipping up on me." I eased my hand down to her back and drew her closer. Our lips melted together. Her arms gently laced around my bandaged torso as her soft breasts pressed against my chest. I felt the butt of my pistol prodding her arm.

Slowly she drew away and glanced at the pistol. "Is that loaded?" she asked apprehensively.

"Sure is," I replied, reaching for my shirt. "Works best that way." I looked up while buttoning my shirt and winked at her.

She turned to face the wall mirror and nonchalantly ran her fingers through her hair. "Do you keep a round chambered?"

The casual tone of her question brought my head up to the mirrored reflection of her face. The fact that a woman could ask something so knowledgeable about firearms stirred me. Tracy, a civilian, had been in 'Nam over ten months, but the only weapon I'd seen her carry was her camera—she snapped a nude shot of me coming out of the shower while we were in Thailand.

"Yes, I keep a round chambered. If the defecation has already hit the cooling apparatus, the time it takes to chamber a round can be too long. But how do you know about all that? Don't tell me you were on the college pistol team!"

Tracy sat down in the visitor's chair and crossed her long legs. "No, but my dad was a pretty good shot. One year while I was home for summer break he took me to a range and taught me how to shoot." She cast a look upward. "I still remember the long emphatic lecture he gave me about firearms safety."

Her eyes returned to mine with a smile. "Of course we were firing a thirty-eight snub-nosed Smith and Wesson revolver at a stationary target, so we didn't have to worry about things like defecation and fans and chambering a round!" She grinned and fluttered her eyelashes.

I felt my mouth gaping and quickly closed it. Inwardly, I was impressed. It seemed the longer I knew Tracy Gibbs, the more my fascination with her grew.

I decided to change the subject from pistols to pleasure. "Did you get us a hotel room?"

Tracy informed me that although she had looked at several other hotels, she soon discovered the one she was already in was the best. Her room had a large French-style bathtub, a veranda, and a beautiful view of Da Nang harbor.

The beautiful view didn't excite me, but the bathtub did. I was looking forward to a rainy night of romance with an enchanting woman I'd grown to love. I really wasn't sure where our paths would lead from here, but I did know that in less than twenty-four hours she was bound for home, and a day later I'd be headed to Zulu.

I wasn't concerned about my destination—it beat hanging around the flagpole with Twitty at CCN. But I knew if Tracy found out about me going into a combat assignment voluntarily, she'd do a low-level back flip over it. She'd already put me through a long rhyme and reason dissertation about my "insane" decision to stay in 'Nam. No, I decided, the less she knew about Hill 950, the better.

I lifted my ruck off the bed and placed it near the door. "How'd your interview with Helen Goodwin go?"

"Very good. It was my last interview and, I think, the best. She's been accepted at the Baylor College of Medicine when she completes her tour of duty here. You know, she really likes you, Brett. If I weren't sure she's well aware you're already taken, I'd be jealous. I think I am, anyhow." She pulled a cigarette from her combination purse and camera case.

"I like Helen too, honey. She reminds me a lot of you. She's professional, she's as hard as woodpecker lips, and personable. And she maintains her sense of femininity. Some of the nurses walk around here with their knuckles dragging the ground."

Tracy laughed. "As hard as woodpecker lips, Yancy. I'm not sure Helen would appreciate that analogy."

Just then, a tall orderly backed slowly through the door pulling a gurney.

"I'm back from my photo session, gang!" Bobby's smiling eyes greeted me, then Tracy. *"Buenos dias, chula."*

Tracy replied in fluent Spanish. *"Buenos dias, guapo."*

While the orderly helped Bobby into bed, they continued talking in Spanish as if nobody else were around. I understood Rod's enthusiasm. Since learning that Tracy spoke Spanish, he enjoyed the opportunity to speak it with her during her daily visits.

I enjoyed listening to their conversations and had even learned some Spanish myself during the past several days. On one occasion, after Tracy had left the room, Rod looked over at me and remarked, "Man, I can't believe your lady speaks such good Spanish. Are you sure she's a gringo?"

• • •

An hour later Dr. Ostman came in to remove my bandages and check me over before signing off on my release. Tracy excused herself during my preflight examination.

The removal of my bandages was a welcome surprise. I hadn't looked forward to spending the last night with Tracy wrapped up like a mummy.

While he was cutting away the gauze wraps around my chest, the good doctor reminded me about my light-duty restrictions. I told him I was beginning to think there was an echo in the hospital.

After he departed I slipped quickly into my shoulder holster and shirt. I was glad to have some private moments with Bobby before Tracy's return. It was an opportunity to try and get some answers from the one man who knew Hill 950 like the sights on his rifle. Without Tracy listening I could talk freely.

I spoke while buttoning my shirt. "Rod, I'm headed up to your neck of the woods in a couple of days, Nine-fifty. I need to know—"

He interrupted me, laughing. "Right, Brett, and I'm heading for a roller-derby fiesta!"

I stepped closer to his bed. "Look, buddy, I don't have much time before Tracy comes back, and I don't want her knowing about this."

"You're serious, man?"

"Like a sucking chest wound. I'm being assigned to a radio-relay slot on Nine-fifty in about two days. You told me the VC are throwing everything but water buffalos at y'all up there. Now, we both know that piss-ant hill isn't worth a handful of rice to Charlie.

"What I need to know is, why in the hell are they dumping so much shit on it? Why are they trying to run the Marines out?"

He placed his unlit cigarette back on his nightstand and pushed himself up in bed. A frown came over his face. "Look, Brett, I've already told you I think you're about three rounds shy of a full magazine for even staying in 'Nam. But, man, if you're letting them put you up on Zulu, you ain't even got—"

"That's beside the point! We're going to have two SF recon teams working that area soon, and I need to know what they're up against, and why?"

Bobby reached for a cigarette and lit it. He took a deep draw and glanced up at me. "Look, man, I don't know the answer. I'm not sure anybody does. All we know is, between hits, there's a lot of night movement north of us toward the 'D.' "

He looked up at the ceiling, then back at me out of the corner of his eye. "But there's a dude up there named Cino. He might know something. He's just been busted from E-four down to three. Insubordination. He's a hard dude, man. Strange, quiet, like there's some kind of fuse burning inside him. At times you can almost hear it when you're near him.

"Anyhow, he worked as a forward observer, solo, along the 'D' for six months, then got assigned to us."

Rod took a draw on his smoke again, narrowing his eyes as if looking back in time. "One stormy night a few weeks back I was on guard duty when I noticed something creeping up the drainage ditch on the south side of the hill—the steep side. At first I thought it was a rat. Shit, we got rats up there the size of pit bulls, man.

"But as I raised my rifle, I saw it was Cino. He'd been out on a solo night patrol—nobody does that! In fact, I'm probably the only one who knows he does it."

Rod paused and looked at me as if to make sure I understood it was privileged info, then continued. "What I'm saying is, if anybody has an idea of what the fuck is going on and why, it's him—Cino Cassidy."

Chapter 4

Tracy pressed close to me in the small back seat of the jostling cab. Her fingers interlaced with mine as our driver bounced us down the water-covered road like a vehicular basketball. The highway into Da Nang city had more potholes than the Ho Chi Minh trail had bomb craters.

The morning storm had subsided to a light drizzle. Now, ebony clouds hung low over the distant mist-shrouded city, threatening heavy rain.

I gazed out the rain-splattered window at the passing jagged mass of dilapidated sheds, tents, and plywood huts lining both sides of the narrow road. Old people squatted beneath shelters. Their somber, empty faces peered silently into the mist watching laughing children at play—kids clinging to their fading childhood in a country at war.

Ahead of us, naked children splashed happily in the shallow canal paralleling the road. Our driver slowed, stopping near them, to await the lazy crossing of a water buffalo. A small boy standing in the canal glanced up from the gathering and waved to us.

Tracy smiled and returned his wave. She spoke as

31

though thinking out loud. "This is the third most prosperous city in South Vietnam, but the people live in shambles surrounded by filth."

Watching the children, I answered: "These are the hut people, darlin'. They're refugees in their own country. They had to run from the Communists. The ones that made it here alive have a simple choice: stay here and try to survive by scavenging and begging, or go back to the countryside, the fields, and face slaughter by the NVA. Some get so destitute they actually—"

Suddenly my eyes caught the thick ripple of a deadly sea snake moving through the water toward the little boy. Bolting from the car, I jerked the Beretta from beneath my shirt. I leveled a quick aim at the dark serpent and fired. My round cracked into the snake's head as children screamed and scurried from the water. I held my aim for a second watching it spasm and jerk, then go limp, floating with its yellow belly up.

I took a deep breath, tucked my pistol away, and watched an old man hobble to the water's edge. He dipped a bamboo stick beneath the snake and raised the limp, blood-dripping serpent from the water.

He smiled through black-stained teeth as he looked across the canal at me, chattering loudly, *"Cho-toi? Cho-toi?"*

I smiled back at him. "Sure, papasan, you can have it. You and the family have a good meal tonight."

As I turned to walk back to the cab the little naked boy hurried to me with his open palm raised upward. At first I thought he wanted money, but looking closer at his palm I noticed something bright. I smiled. He had picked up the expended cartridge from my pistol and was returning it to me.

I bowed, then knelt on one knee facing him and accepted the cartridge. Looking into his dark eyes, I spoke softly. "*Cam on*, thank you. *Ten-toi la*, Yancy. *Ten-em?*"

His voice rose proudly, telling me his name. "Phung, Phung Tran." He poked his small hand toward me, imitating American custom.

I accepted his handshake. "Phung Tran. Number one. How old are you?"

"Phung Tran! *Lai dai! Lai dai!*"

My eyes followed his to see a woman wearing a sloping straw hat standing near a hut. She glared at us with a hands-on-hips stance. Some gestures are internationally common. As a kid, I'd seen that get-your-ass-home look myself more than a few times.

I quickly pulled a ten piaster bill from my shirt and handed it to Phung Tran. I motioned toward the cartridge in my hand, implying the money was for the return of it—not charity.

He smiled, bowed, and hurried away toward his mother.

As I stood and walked toward the car, a thought hit me. Now, what if that little fellow starts thinking every expended shell he finds is worth ten piasters. He's in for a rude awakening if he tries to cash them in like I used to do with pop bottles.

I whispered to myself, "You think too much, Yancy. It was the right thing to do."

Sliding back onto the seat next to Tracy, I closed the door and motioned for the driver to press on.

I gave Tracy a pseudo-serious look. "I hope you don't mind, Tracer. I let that old man have the snake without asking if you wanted it."

Tracy leaned away from me slightly with a silent questioning look. Her words came slowly. "Yancy, you are incredible. In fact, if I was prone to profanity, I'd say in-fucking-credible. But, no, I don't want the snake. I never have liked—''

I interrupted her, smiling. ''Prone, prone? You know, there's something about that word I like. Driver! *Le len*, Da Nang!''

By 1300 hours Tracy and I were sitting in the near-empty second-floor restaurant of her hotel finishing lunch. Gusting rain pelted the large French-style windows near our table, obscuring the view of Da Nang harbor.

I pushed back from the table and relaxed while sipping a Jim Beam and Coke as Tracy finished the last bites of her shark steak. Throughout the meal we'd both been quiet. I reasoned it was because of our preoccupation with her departure tomorrow, as well as what the days and weeks ahead would bring. Could our love stand a time test?

As Tracy lit a cigarette I sensed she was on the same thought frequency as me.

Her soft, melancholy words confirmed it. ''I haven't even left here and I miss you already.''

I reached across the table and wiped a pending tear from her eye. I could have easily spoken the same words to her. But our last moments didn't need to be hindered with the burden of worry. I smiled into her gleaming eyes while my mind struggled to find some words to comfort her.

''Tracer, I don't know how true it is, but they say 'Absence makes the heart grow fonder.' I feel like I'm probably going to enjoy pizza a lot more when I get back home.''

It worked. She cast a lopsided grin at me. ''Yancy, how dare you compare missing me with a pizza!'' She paused and took a contemplative draw on her smoke, then added, "But I've heard another version, absence is to love as the wind is to a flame; it extinguishes the small and fans the large. If that's true, we'll know in the weeks to come." She leaned forward. "You know, you don't have to stay here. It's not too late to change your—"

"Tracy, we've been through all that, darlin'. I don't—"

"Waiter!" She turned her head, ignoring me as a white-jacketed young man hurried to the table and bowed. "Give me one of those please." She pointed toward my drink.

"Them mot," I said, raising my empty glass.

Tracy remained silent until our drinks arrived. Then, she raised the glass to her mouth and took a long drink. The drink was immediately followed by a grimace and a strange, low groan.

I tried not to laugh, but it didn't work. I'd neglected to tell her I was drinking doubles, so naturally the waiter, following orders, brought her the same thing. I raised a hand to cover my mouth.

"Don't you laugh, Yancy!" she said, reaching for her water glass.

Recovering from the heavy Jim Beam taste shock, she began sipping her drink slowly. Her eyes watched me as if looking for any signs of a chuckle, and to let me know she wasn't backing down.

After several sips and a long silence she leaned forward and crushed her cigarette into the ashtray. "Brett, staying in Vietnam when you don't have to does not make sense. Maybe it's selfish of me to try and change your mind, but I love you, and I don't just fall in love every millennium." She leaned back in her chair as if to say, "I rest my case."

During the past week Tracy had heard all of my reasons for staying in 'Nam. Nothing seemed to get through to her. Now, it was time to let her hear from someone else.

I reached into my shirt pocket and withdrew a letter. I spoke while unfolding it. ''I received this from Will's wife yesterday. I'd like to share it with you.'' Tracy nodded.

I read:

''Dear Brett,

''Thank you so much for your letter and for returning Will's belongings so soon. It is comforting for us to hold those things that were papa's. Even now, the kids and I touch his clothes and his pictures, and we read through that old shoe box full of our letters that he saved up. Each thing is sacred to us. I don't know how we would make it without them. It's like being with him again.

''Tonight, as I write to you, I can see little Karen, she's our youngest, in the parlor, cuddled up in papa's chair. She's reading one of his letters to her. William always wrote a separate letter to each of the kids ever month, like to kinda let each one of them know they was special to him. Karen likes to go to sleep in that raggedy old chair holding one of his letters and sometimes the one you wrote us. It's a wonder we ain't wore that letter of your's out by now.

''Karen asked me yesterday if I wrote back to Brett Yancy yet. I told her, no not yet. Well, she hugged up to me and asked me to write and tell you that she loves you.

"I'm sorry it's taken me so long to write. For the longest I couldn't do nothing. I tried to write but it seemed like my hand trembled ever time the pen touched the paper and all I could think about was the aching emptiness of life without my man.

"You know, Will talked about you a lot in his letters to us. He thought the world of you, and I think us knowing that there's a man who papa loved and respected over there taking up where he left off is one of those blessings in disguise that helps us keep the faith here at home.

"I close this letter now. Please remember we all love you Sergeant Yancy and that you are in our prayers every night. I will write again soon.

> "Love and faith,
> Chunky Washington

"P.S. I always sent papa a little box of oatmeal or sugar cookies ever other week. If you don't mind, I'd like to keep that habit for a while and send them to you. It would be kinda like still doing something loving for William."

I tucked the letter back into my pocket and gazed out at the rainy sky. "You know what his favorite song was? Did I ever tell you?"

Tracy pulled a napkin to her eyes, then reached to touch my arm. "Yes, honey. You told me while we were in Thailand. 'The Twelfth of Never,' by Johnny Mathis . . . Thank you for sharing the letter with me. It's beautiful, and it's what I needed to help me understand."

I breathed a deep sigh, then smiled at her. "I think I hear some warm flowing water and a big French bathtub calling me. How about we adjourn to the room and share a bath?'' I winked. "Saves water, you know.''

Tracy smiled and reached for her purse. "Waiter, check please.''

As the waiter approached with the check, Tracy withdrew a twenty-dollar bill and started to hand it to him.

"Hold on, Tracer,'' I said, quickly reaching into my pocket. I placed a thousand piaster note in his hand and gestured for him to keep the change.

"Is this your way of invoking chauvinism, monsieur? I was going to pay for—''

"It's not chauvinism at all, honey,'' I said, lifting my drink to finish it. "I just didn't want any more of our greenbacks headed to Hanoi. And that's exactly where they go. They end up using our currency to finance their war.''

Tracy tilted her head slightly. "Could you run that by me again, handsome? They use our money?''

I placed my glass back on the table. "Yes. They use our money. The economics boils down to this. The North Vietnamese have to buy war materials. But, on the world market, their currency is on a par with Monopoly money. So, they pay top price, four times the regular exchange rate of piasters to green on the black market for every American dollar they can get their greasy little fingers on.''

Tracy's brow furrowed in shock and amazement. "Are you saying that all this time I've been here, I've been indirectly supporting the NVA?''

"Roger that. But it's more like 'directly.' It's not your fault. It's our demented State Department. Their policy of allowing American civilians here to use green is flat-ass stupid!

"And if you look deeper, it doesn't take a large brain

to see why a lot of Vietnamese businessmen and government officials don't want this war to end. They're getting rich on it. In fact, a lot of our American civilian support types are making a bundle too. If one of them brings in, say, fifty thousand dollars, he can double it overnight on the black market money exchange. The NVA also buy all the gold they can, because gold stands up anywhere.''

She leaned forward, touching my arm. ''Wait a minute, Brett. I know for a fact that the Soviets and the Chinese Communists are supplying weapons to the NVA. So if all this is true, why does Hanoi need so much purchasing power?''

''What you're saying is only partially true, Tracer. Yes, the NVA's main suppliers are the Soviets. But they're not getting a free ride. Sure, they're getting bargain basement prices, but they still have to pay. Also, there're a lot of items the Soviets can't supply that the North has to buy on the world market. Grain, medical supplies, and rubber, to name just a few.''

''Okay, how about military payment certificates? I thought that was supposed to be a form of currency control?''

''It is, but the American military is the only group that has to conform to it.'' I pulled a ten-dollar MPC note from my shirt pocket. ''This bill has the same value as a greenback in *South Vietnam*. Now, another surprise. Even it can be converted at a rate of two to one, MPC to green, on the black market. So if a soldier has a friend back home send him 'X' amount of green, the soldier can double the money again, overnight. The field troops don't do it because they don't have easy access to the cities. It's the stay-behind garrison troops that can get away with it. And you have to remember that most of the American soldiers here are in noncombat jobs and do have ready access to the black market.''

Tracy drew a hand slowly to her chin. "Okay, let's say that happens. This guy can't send MPC back home. What does he do with it all?''

"He simply goes to one of the military post offices, buys a money order using MPC, and sends it home to his friend.''

Tracy frowned. "Doesn't that raise some eyebrows when a soldier starts sending home twice as much as he's earning here? I mean, everybody can't say they've been winning big in the poker games.''

"You're absolutely right. So that helps curb people from getting too greedy. It's the feet-up-on-the-desk finance officers that are making the big hauls. They don't have anybody looking over their shoulders. They justify all their exchanges by ledgering them as money used for R and R conversions. Since everybody goes on at least one R and R, there's a lot of green allocated for that purpose.''

"Brett, this is incredible! But I know you're not dreaming this up. So let me ask, how do you know all this to be true?''

I stood and held my hand out to her. "Can we continue this on the way to the room? I can still hear that bath beckoning me.''

Tracy stood and slipped her arm around me as we walked slowly toward the room.

"About six months back Will and I had to go down to Saigon for a mission debriefing at SOG headquarters. While I was there I went downtown one night to''—I paused, trying to assemble a more palatable phrase for "get laid"—"to, partake of some commercial affection .''

"Oh, get laid,'' she said matter-of-factly.

"Yeah, well, I ran into this fat captain in one of the bars on Tudo Street. Wingate was his name. Anyhow, the good *dai 'uy* was about three sheets to the wind and started buying me drinks. At first I thought he was queer, the way he kept smiling at me and looking up at my beret.

"Then he begins telling me his life story. He said he was airborne-qualified and wanted to be a Green Beret, but somehow he got put in the finance corps because he was an accounting graduate. I didn't doubt his assignment with finance, he was wearing finance brass on his khakis and had a pocket full of pens, but he was lying about being airborne."

Tracy turned her head toward me. "How could you tell?"

"Only takes one question, Tracer. I asked him how many PLFs he carried on a night jump. He answered five." I looked at Tracy's puzzled expression and grinned. "A PLF is a parachute landing fall. You don't carry them on a jump, it's what you do when you hit the ground. A Leg, a nonjumper, just cannot bullshit a jumper."

By the time we'd reached the room I'd explained to Tracy that the captain had poured his schnockered soul out to me. He'd boasted he was making so much money on the black market money exchange that he could buy me women and booze for an entire tour of duty and never put a dent in his wallet. It quietly pissed me off when he implied I was stupid for not getting in on the "big bucks bandwagon." I restrained the urge to impale his fat face on a long bamboo straw—choosing instead to ask smiling questions about his method of operation and contact points. The next day I made a full detailed report to an

Army Criminal Investigation Division officer. The CID loves to nail extortionists.

A few steps from the room, Tracy halted abruptly and whispered, "Brett, look! The door's open."

"Yeah?" I said.

"Yes, and I know I locked it."

I instructed Tracy to wait while I moved forward to check the room. Easing cautiously inside, I scanned the large room, then walked to the veranda entrance and peered out the French doors at the rain-splattered court. Gazing at the street below, I noticed a thick trail of vines against the gray stucco walls abutting the patio. Dark water cascaded down the vines like a waterfall fed by a broken rain gutter above them. I slid the unlocked bolt on the door closed.

After checking the bathroom, I shouted, "It's okay, Tracer!"

No answer.

I hurried back to the door and found Tracy kneeling, touching the hallway carpet. "It's wet," she said, looking up at me. "And look, see the dark impression here at the door entrance?"

She stood and walked hurriedly into the room. She checked her camera, portable typewriter, then the bureau drawers.

"Nothing missing," she said, pacing to the patio doors. Looking out the door windows, she said, "Whoever was here must have climbed up those vines, somehow unlocked these doors, and then left through the hallway door. My guess is, he was barefooted."

I moved to Tracy's side and looked toward the watery mass of tangled vines. "Well, Sherlock, if somebody came up that way he had to have scuba gear." I looked closer at the adjacent patio. It was about a six-foot jump to ours. "But someone could have leapt across to here. He wouldn't have to be a track star to do that. And, by the way, these doors weren't locked."

"Yes they were! I'm very security conscious. I had a camera stolen while I was in Nha Trang, and I—"

Turning, I gently pulled her into my embrace and kissed her forehead. "Well, whoever it was didn't get anything. They're gone now, and we're here." I stroked the soft hair on her neck.

Her lips melted into mine as her arms laced around me. The distant rumble of monsoon thunder blended briefly with the pelting beat of rain against the windows.

Through slow breaths I whispered, "Darlin', if you'll draw us a hot bath, I'll call down and order a bottle of champagne, maybe two."

Dipping her tongue into my ear, she whispered back, "Sounds delightful. Ask them if they can bring us a candle. We'll have a candlelight bath together." She drew slowly back, looking up at me. "I've never had a candlelight bath with a man. Have you?"

I narrowed my eyes as though thinking, then gave her a half grin. "No, honey, I never had one with a man, either."

A waiter arrived within moments of my call with two bottles of cold champagne. Earlier, I'd noticed an antique candelabrum sitting on a stand at the end of the hall. I handed the waiter a generous tip and pointed toward the candelabrum, asking if I could borrow it for the evening.

The small man turned and scurried down the hall to retrieve the holder. Returning, he set it on the floor and squatted to carefully light each of the four candles. I really didn't need the candles lit, but I understood Vietnamese service custom. They assumed that if you had ordered something and provided a good tip, it was their duty to make sure it was in full working order when they gave it to you.

I set the champagne and glasses aside and waited while he completed the lighting procedure. Finally, he stood and handed me the glowing candle holder. He then began muttering rapid-fire Vietnamese while pointing at the candles. The words were spoken too fast for me to understand them.

I nodded, saying, *"Merci beaucoup,"* then closed the door.

Walking into the bathroom, I saw Tracy leaning over the tub. "How's this for atmosphere?" I said, placing it on the sink counter.

Tracy reached and turned off the bathroom light. "Oh, that's perfect. Your bath awaits, monsieur." Slowly she began unbuttoning my shirt. Flickers of candlelight danced through the darkness.

She slid the shirt back over my shoulders and off. As I removed my shoulder holster I watched her eyes scan over my chest. It was the first time she'd seen my wounds. Her gentle fingers moved slowly over the furrowed scars.

"You've healed well, honey. You're as beautiful as—"

The loud intrusion of knocks on the door interrupted her.

I reached for my Beretta and paced to the door. *"Ai-do?"*

"Thai, thai," a voice answered. It sounded like the service waiter.

I opened the door to see his face beaming at me. He reached forward to hand me a fistful of long white candles.

I tipped him again and returned to the bathroom. "That was the candle resupply courier, darlin'. He must think we're going to have an all-night seance in here."

"Sounds like a great idea to me. You get into the tub. I'll be right back."

I poured a glass of champagne, took a long sip, then removed my clothes and eased slowly into the deep, steaming pool. Smiling, I leaned back and closed my eyes. The warm relaxing water flooded my senses.

Lying in the dim silence, a caravan of memories drifted slowly through me. Memories of home, my family, my friends, and, strangely, Christmas. I'd be home this year for Christmas. But what kind of Christmas would it be for Will's family? Empty. Empty, cold, and lonely.

My eyes opened to stare at the jagged flickers of light cutting through the darkness. My mind stumbled back to the agonizing memory of Will's body being slammed into the tangled grass by rivets of lead.

Now, the question that had echoed inside me since his death pounded through me again like the unrelenting strike of a hammer against an anvil. Why had I been spared? Why was I still alive when Will had been cut down—snatched away from his family.

And why the fuck was I lying in a goddamn hot bath, enjoying the love of a woman, the taste of champagne, and the luxury of freedom and sweet life?

William Washington was twice the man I'd ever be. He was a good husband—faithful. He was a good father—did without necessities so he could provide for his family. He spent his money buying clothes, food, and presents for his children.

I spent my money to supplement my fucking ego—
cars, leather coats, a new shotgun when I wanted one.

Will hunted with an old gun passed down to him by
his dad. Will brought his game home to feed his family.
But I hunted for trophies to hang on my wall—something
else to augment my ego.

I admired Will. I respected him. But I never knew how
much I truly loved him until I held his limp, blood-soaked
body and cried.

I thought back to the book he'd given me for my birthday—*The Prophet*. It was Will's special book. ''Almost as
important as the Bible,'' he once told me.

He wrote a note about friendship on the cover page.
'' 'When you part from your friend, grieve not; for that
which you love most in him may be clearer in his absence, as the mountain to the climber is clearer from the
plain.'—Kahlil Gibran.''

Tracy's voice brought me back to the present. ''May
I wash your back?''

I turned and watched her fill the glasses with champagne. She wore a white terry bathrobe. The short garment revealed slender, tanned legs. The snugly tied belt
accented her small waist and rounded buttocks.

She handed me a full glass, then sat on the wide edge
of the tub and touched her glass gently to mine. ''To us,
and more of us,'' she whispered.

While we drank my mind lingered on the words,
''More of us.'' I couldn't help thinking the words implied she was planning a family with me. For the first
time the thought did not seem alien.

As she leaned to kiss me I set my glass aside and carefully moved my hand over her waist while tasting the
champagne on her lips.

I slowly loosened her robe and slid my fingers to her

breast, then lightly teased the nipple. Locked in kisses, I drew her slowly back into the warm water and over me.

"Brett . . . Brett," her labored whisper pleaded. "My, my robe, it's—"

Chapter 5

By 1830 hours Tracy and I sat beneath the bright orange canopy of an outdoor restaurant eating *pho*—seaweed soup. A mingled parade of Buddhist monks, soldiers, and Vietnamese ambled through the wet streets near us dodging cycles, mopeds, and taxis. The heavy rain had again subsided to a fine mist, but the evening sun remained buried behind dark clouds.

Da Nang's stink, previously cloaked by the rain, now oozed through the damp air like the vapor from an outhouse. The ancient harbor, a few blocks from where we sat, had a lot to do with the odor. It was contaminated with everything from decayed bodies and sewage to garbage, diesel fuel, and rotted fish. The strong wind blowing in off the South China Sea, across the harbor, brought the stink into every corner and crevice of the city.

The irritated look on Tracy's face told me the odor was starting to bother her.

I took a sip of beer and leaned back in the chair. "If you light a cigarette and exhale the smoke through your nose, it'll help, Tracer. Temporarily, anyhow."

She gave me a dubious look, then lit a cigarette and exhaled the smoke as I'd suggested. After a moment she sniffed the air carefully. "It works. But how did you know that? You're not a smoker."

"Binkowski told me about it. The only problem is that it doesn't last long, unless you're a chain smoker."

"Never smoked chains, Yancy. They're too hard to light. Brett, see that soldier over there carrying those boots?" She pointed toward a tall American walking with a Vietnamese girl. A new pair of U.S.-issue jungle boots swung at his side as he carried them by the tied laces.

"Why would he need an extra pair of boots with him in town?"

"He doesn't. He probably just came from the local market and bought them to send home to a friend. Those boots sell for about four hundred eighty piasters, or four dollars MPC. Of course it's black market trade, but since possession is nine tenths of the law, Army CID doesn't confiscate American issue items, unless they happen to be weapons or ammunition.

"A big portion of the money that soldier just spent on those boots will be used to buy green for Hanoi. It's crazy, but he's supporting the enemy.

"We Americans just can't resist a bargain. Let's take a walk down to the market and I'll show you some more bargains on U.S. goods."

Tracy quickly grabbed her large purse and pulled the camera out. "Wait a minute while I load some film. There's a story in this. If I can get some documentation, it'll make the front page in every newspaper in the country, I'll bet."

I really hadn't planned to trip her trigger on the subject of illegal contraband. And I didn't think a news story was going to change what had been occurring in 'Nam for years—black market trade. Nonetheless, Tracy was a reporter. I knew she was going to pursue a story whether I liked it or not.

Walking through the crowded streets toward the central market, Tracy hit me with a barrage of questions about how the black market acquired American goods in the first place.

I dodged the questions, telling her the information was top secret. She gave it her best shot trying to pry the information out of me. When that didn't work, she got mad.

In the midst of the crowd she stopped in her tracks. "Brett, how in God's name do you expect me to expose this graft and corruption if you won't cooperate? I will guarantee you complete anonymity, but I've got to—"

"Dammit, Tracer . . ." I yanked my beret off and looked skyward, then glared back at her. I didn't want a pissing contest started on our last day together. Inwardly, I admired her devotion to truth. And I admired her courage. But I knew that any story about military corruption or, in this case, military stupidity could put her pretty head on the block.

Her eyes told me she didn't give a damn about jeopardy and consequence when they came to odds with her desire to get a story.

"Okay, okay," I said, motioning her forward. I put my beret on and slipped my arm over her shoulder, glancing from side to side briefly as I spoke.

"I can't tell you how all the American goods end up on the black market, but I can tell you how ten thousand pairs of jungle boots got there.

"Several months back some mental giant colonel at SOG headquarters got the bright idea that NVA trackers couldn't track our recon teams in Laos and Cambodia if they were wearing the same boots we wear. His reasoning was good. If the trails were all marked up with their tracks, they couldn't distinguish our tracks from theirs—"

"Wait! NVA wear Bata boots. Even I know that. So why—"

"Dammit, Tracer! Don't ask questions. Just listen. Anyhow, his reasoning was right on target. The NVA, given the choice, would prefer our boots to the cheap tennis shoe–type foot gear they're issued. So, some general authorized SOG to dump ten thousand new pairs of our jungle boots all along the Ho Chi Minh trail on a low-level night drop. Great idea, huh?"

"Sounds reasonable. So, what's the catch?"

"Well, somewhere in the course of this *Star Trek* scenario, the good colonel somehow forgot that the NVA have little feet. They dumped sizes ten, eleven, and twelve! Long story short, the NVA couldn't wear them so they ended up in every black market from Quang Tri to Can Tho being sold back to GIs at four dollars a pair!"

Tracy stopped abruptly. I could almost hear the wheels of her methodical mind turning. "That's incredible," she muttered.

"No, Tracer. What's that special word of yours? It's . . . in-fuckin'-credible."

"Yancy, do you realize that comes to forty thousand dollars we have given them?"

"Roger, providing all the boots sell, which is unlikely. But it still amounts to a lot of money we've given them. Not to mention what the boots cost the American taxpayer in the first place."

She turned to face me. "Brett, how do you know this to be factual?"

"Know what to be factual?"

"What you just told me about this classified boot mission."

"I don't remember telling you anything, darlin'. Besides, I'm not authorized to divulge classified information." I winked. "Understand?"

"Roger, understand," she said with a fading smile.

A few steps later, we entered the crowded marketplace. The steady drone of chatter drifted through the narrow congested aisle along with the smells of dead fish, marijuana, opium, and urine.

Old people squatted near their cluttered stalls waving callused hands, yelling for us to come and see their assortment of fruit, vegetables, trinkets, and drugs. Children pawed at our arms showing us watches, knives, Buddha figurines, and scarfs.

A young boy walked backward in front of us. He held a plastic strip of nude female pictures. "Number one Vietnamese for you, Joe."

I glanced to the rear, then back to Tracy. "Watch your purse, Tracer. I don't feel up to a hundred-yard dash today."

Tracy huddled close to me as we edged slowly through the mingled odor of people, smoke, and flies.

Near a bend in the aisle Tracy stopped and looked down at the dwarfed figure of a double amputee. The old Vietnamese soldier wore a frayed fatigue shirt. His hand trembled as he raised a tin cup toward us.

His shrill voice chattered loudly above the noise of the crowd. *"Sat cong. Sat cong."*

Tracy took some piasters from her purse and placed them into the cup. "What's he saying?"

I looked down into his weathered face. "Death to the Communists. That's what he's saying." I glanced at the faded shoulder patch on his shirt. The green-and-white emblem depicted a tiger leaping across an open parachute with three lightning bolts below it. It was the symbol of the Vietnamese Special Forces.

I pulled a five-hundred-piaster bill from my pocket and stuffed it in the cup. *"Sat-cong, papasan."*

I turned to Tracy. "This is how the South Vietnamese government repays its disabled patriots. They allow them begging privileges."

"Cam on, cam on," the man chattered while bowing his head.

Turning, Tracy squinted through the haze. "Brett, I haven't seen any military goods here. Are you sure this is the right place?"

I pointed beyond the old man. "Follow me. They're back here. Get your camera ready. They're not going to be smiling for you, so be quick about it."

Tracy readied the camera as we moved through a thick cloud of opium smoke.

I coughed as the acrid haze pierced my senses. My right elbow pressed against the Beretta hanging beneath my armpit. I didn't like being here, particularly with a woman, and more particularly with a woman taking pictures of contraband.

"My God! It's like a huge Army and Navy store in here!"

As we moved along the rows and stacks of boots, packs, machetes, and fatigues I felt that sixth sense nudge me. Something was watching us and it was near.

"You about finished, Tracer?"

"Just a few more shots."

Suddenly a hideous screech pierced the air. Claws gripped my shoulders. I spun driving my clinched fist into the attacker. The furry length of a tail lashed my face as the dark creature fell away from me and scampered across a pile of blankets. Recovering my breath, I heard Tracy's chiding voice.

"Oh, Brett! That's the cutest little monkey. I hope you didn't hurt him!" She quickly raised her camera to take a picture of it. "Can we buy monkeys here somewhere?"

"Tracy, you may find this a little hard to understand, but I don't like fucking monkeys! Let's go this way," I said, taking her hand.

"Where are we going?"

"There's a place over here that sells American liquor. I'm going to buy a bottle of Jim Beam."

"But, Brett, won't that be supporting the . . . Never mind."

During our exit from the market I noticed we were being followed by two Vietnamese police—Quan canh.

The QC were as arrogant as the Nazi SS and as corrupt as Mexican Federales. They tolerated the Korean troops here, but made no secret of their contempt for American and Australian soldiers. They had the often-abused authority to kill anyone they suspected of antigovernment activity, on the spot, no questions asked. And they could twist the definition of antigovernment activity any way they wanted to.

I'd had a run-in with them one night several months back while I was downtown getting my sperm count lowered. Fortunately Swede Jensen, another One-Zero from camp, had been with me that night. After we showed the QC our passes, they started in with a line of bullshit to try and intimidate us.

Jensen, who had a fuse about the size of a match head, finally lit up one of his Eastwood-type cigars, blew a cloud of smoke in their faces, and butted in, saying, "Evidently you little pricks never heard of Southern hospitality. Here you are carrying rifles given to you by my country, driving a jeep from my country, and we're over here getting our asses shot at trying to beat the Communists off you.

"You little assholes are tryin' to piss down our back and tell us it's raining."

We left them standing there with their mouths gaping. We laughed about it later, but we both knew they could have cut us down and gotten away with it.

Tracy leaned close and whispered in my ear, "I think those policemen are following us."

A few steps from the hotel one shouted, "*Dung lai!* Halt!"

Turning to face them, I remembered seeing the pair in the market area. One man held his rifle on us while the other looked Tracy up and down. He spoke directly to her, ignoring me.

"You go markee but you no buy nothing. Why you takee picture? Why you come Vietnam?"

Now it became clear to me why they were following. They were evidently providing protection for the black market and didn't want any photographs getting out.

Tracy answered him while removing a press pass from her purse. "I'm an American journalist. Surely you understand that journalists take pictures."

He examined her pass, then handed it back to her. "You can no takee pictures markee. Giving me camera!"

He reached for the strap of Tracy's purse. I moved quickly between them and seized his wrist. "You're not taking a damn thing, asshole! This lady's with me." I heard the sharp snap of a rifle bolt behind me.

A loud voice bellowed through the wind. "What's the goddamn problem here?"

I turned to see a heavy black major lumbering toward us. He looked like a reincarnation of Leroy Brown. The unlit stub of a cigar stayed clamped in his teeth as he leered at the QC in my grip.

A CID identification card hung from the shirt pocket of his khaki uniform. He barked again: "I said, 'What's the goddamn problem here,' boy?"

I released my grip as the QC began jabbering up at the big major. For some reason he had forgotten his English. After listening to the muttering for a moment, the major interrupted him. A second later the pair saluted and left.

The major flipped the cigar stub into the street, glanced back at the retreating QC, then turned to us. "Y'all been down to the market, I see." He glanced at the sack in my hand. "And you been taking pictures down there."

Tracy started to reach into her purse again. "Yes, that's right. I'm a journalist and—"

"No need to show me anything. There ain't no law against taking pictures down there. Those little turkeys are just tryin' to stir up trouble. It's their favorite pastime. How much longer you gonna be in Da Nang?"

"I'm leaving to go back Stateside tomorrow."

"Well, that's just as well. Try and stay clear of those little pricks . . . I mean turkeys, till you get outa here. The bastards can get away with murder here, and I mean that literally."

He turned, glancing at my beret. "What SF outfit you with?"

"Command and Control North, out by Marble Mountain."

"Yeah! CCN, I know y'all's commander out there. Colonel Kahn. Good man. He helped us out during Tet.

Brought a whole kick-ass hatchet force in here to help us mop up some VC.''

I saluted. "Thanks for the assist here, sir. For a minute I thought I was going to have to smear this Jim Beam over that boy's skull."

He laughed. "Jim Beam! Man, that's good liquor. It can make a fella trip over matchsticks and step over telephone poles." He shifted the rifle and pulled out another cigar. "I gotta get. I'm playing duty officer tonight. Tell Colonel Kahn, Big Earl Wheeler said hi. Y'all be careful."

As we watched him walk down the windy street, Tracy said, "I wonder why those CQs didn't try and stop us in the market? Why did they wait and follow us?"

"They're QC, Tracer, not CQ. They probably didn't want a confrontation there with other GIs in the area. And they might have wanted to find out where we were staying. Black market is big business here, darlin'. They didn't want to shit in their own mess kit."

"What did you say? Shit in their mess kit?"

"Just a term, Tracer; military term, that is."

Bright flashes of lightning illuminated the sky over our patio like a short-circuited strobe light flickering through the rainy night.

"What a great story this is going to be." Tracy spoke as though talking to her typewriter. Her fingers danced over the keys while she sat at the table. Occasionally she stopped to glance upward as if picking a thought from an invisible tree of ideas.

Clad only in a towel, I sipped my Beam and leaned back against the headboard of the bed. This wasn't exactly how I'd envisioned spending our last night together. I looked at my watch—2130.

"How's your drink, Tracer?"

She reached and took a sip from her near-empty glass. "I'll have another. I'm almost finished here. I'll read this to you in just a minute."

"Great."

The dull tone of my word stopped her. "Brett, honey, I know this isn't very romantic of me, but I need to get this down while it's all fresh in my mind."

I looked into her eyes. For the past eleven months Tracy Gibbs had been rooting through every nut and bolt of this war, writing and sending stories back home about the men fighting here. She'd volunteered for this assignment. She'd given up comfort and luxury, security and safety, to come here for one thing: the American journalists' commitment to truth.

Suddenly it dawned on me that I was being just a little hypocritical. One of the things I loved about her was her dedication. But, now, I was trying to have her put all that aside for my selfish desire.

I stood and walked to the table. "Tracy Gibbs, it occurs to me that if I was writing an operations order for an important mission, you wouldn't bug me while I was working on it. Am I right or wrong?"

Her head tilted slightly. "Roger, Brett Yancy. You're right."

I winked. "Enough said. You take your time, darlin'. I'll mix us another Beam."

Two Beams later I'd finished reading back to back *Newsweek* articles. One about another hippie demonstration against war and killing, the other about the brutal slaying of Sharon Tate at her home in California by a group of hippies.

The silence of the typewriter brought my attention back to Tracy.

"Finished. And once I do some edit and polish on this, it will be outstanding. I hope this does some good."

"Send a copy to General Abrams. That'll make his day," I said wryly.

"He'll see it soon enough. I can promise you that."

She turned off the table lamp, then stood and finished her drink while glancing over my body. She set the glass down, then walked over to the bed and turned out the nightstand light. Slowly she removed her robe and let it fall to the floor.

My eyes roved over her nude body as she looked down at me. She whispered, "I can feel the amber current stirring my libidinous spirit, monsieur. Will you make love to me?"

As she eased gently down over me a flash of monsoon lightning glistened over her hair.

"Brett, wake up. I hear something."

I felt a hand grip my shoulder as she whispered again— more urgently this time.

"Brett, someone is in our—"

Suddenly the something hard slammed into my head. Again it struck. A body straddled me. I struggled to rise, feeling the coarse texture of wood vising my neck. A panicked flicker of memory flashed through me. I'd known this helpless feeling before in a martial-arts class.

Nunchuckus!

The powerful clamp bit into my flesh as I grappled blindly over my head, trying to clutch the hair of my attacker. The crushing jaws locked tighter around my neck, numbing my senses—my strength faded.

A voice screamed through the darkness. "Stop it! Stop or I'll shoot!"

The sharp burst of gunfire splintered the air. Again it cracked.

I felt the weight fall away, freeing me from its death grip. Blinking, gasping, I tried to rise. Naked warmth pressed against me. "Brett! Oh, Brett! Are you all right? Please say—"

"I'm . . . I'm okay," I said weakly while rubbing my neck. I reached to turn on a lamp and sat on the edge of the bed. My squinting eyes moved over the black-clad VC sprawled on the floor near me.

Tracy's rounds were well placed—one neck shot, one shot to the temple. Nunchuckus lay beside the body. I turned to gently take the Beretta from Tracy and place it on the nightstand.

She slowly drew the twisted bed sheet up to her chin. "Is he . . . is he dead?"

I stood and nudged my foot against his bloody head. "Dead enough!"

Mist-laced wind swirled through the open veranda doors. I moved to close the doors, then turned and saw Tracy pull the sheet to her face.

I knelt in front of her and pulled her into my embrace. I listened to her whimpers. She needed to cry for a while. But soon she'd need something else—reasoning. Reasoning to try and justify the most horrible act a human can commit—the killing of another. I knew that gut-quaking agony. It surged through your soul with the wrath of a sickle—slashing and obliterating that precious inner core of virtue and innocence we all cling to for sanity.

Strangely, the words of Will Washington echoed through my mind. "Once we kill, no matter what the need or reason, we're never the same again. Never."

Loud knocks and shouts hammered at the door.

Tracy's tearstained face looked up at me. "I feel sick. I don't want to see anyone."

I wrapped the sheet carefully around her and helped her into the bathroom. Pulling a chair into the room I sat her down near the commode.

"I'll be back."

I moved to the hallway door and opened it. A mixed crowd of servants, Army MPs, and Vietnamese stepped back abruptly as they looked at me.

Glancing down, I realized that I was still naked.

Chapter 6

A skinny MP lieutenant carrying a swagger stick was the first one into the room. He looked down at the VC's head lying in a dark puddle of blood and immediately drew the hand holding the stick up to his mouth, poking himself squarely in the eye.

A moment later the junior version of Patton ordered a sergeant to take charge, then left. I asked the sergeant to get Major Earl Wheeler on the scene.

After discovering Tracy's camera missing, Major Wheeler theorized that two VC had entered the room with the intention of recovering the pictures Tracy had taken of the black market.

Nguyen Nunchuckus, the silent kill specialist, was evidently supposed to put my lights out while the other searched for the camera. What they hadn't counted on was quick-draw Tracer. Fortunately, I had placed my Beretta on the nightstand before going to bed. More fortunately, Tracy didn't fuck around about using it.

An hour later Tracy and I were relocated in another room where she lay restlessly in my arms for the remainder of the night.

It wasn't until morning that I discovered the VC intruders had lost on both counts. While one of them had managed to escape with the camera—he didn't get the film. Tracy had removed the film after our return from the market.

It was my amused guess that the local VC had now attained a new, anguished respect for American "markswoman-ship." They lost one VC, KIA, and all they had to show for it was a well-used Minolta camera.

With tears in her eyes and the roaring prop blast of the C-130 dancing through her hair, Tracy Gibbs waved farewell from across the windswept runway.

I held my beret in one hand and squinted into the stinging cloud of sand. I forced a smile while waving back to her as a flight-suited loadmaster yelled for her to board. She walked up the tailgate into the cavernous darkness of the aircraft, then turned and slowly mouthed the words, "I love you," while waving. The ramp rose and she was gone.

I stood in the morning sunlight and watched her plane hurl down the runway, then rise and slowly disappear into a cloud-patched southern sky. As I gazed at the fading speck of her plane, part of me felt relieved that she was leaving Vietnam. In two hours she'd be boarding a Pan Am flight at Cam Ranh Bay and heading home to safety. Another part of me wished I was going with her. I loved Tracy Gibbs, and I didn't have to flip back through too many pages of my life to realize the happiest moments I'd known were the ones spent with her.

I turned and walked back toward the jeep where Earl Wheeler waited. He'd insisted on driving us to the airport. "Just in case mister Charles is thinkin' 'bout messin' with y'all again."

I slid into the right-side seat, put my beret on, and took a last glance at the empty southern sky.

Wheeler's strong voice spoke to me like a dad talking to his son. "That's a fine woman, that Tracy. It really ain't none of my business, you understand, but if it was me, I don't think I'd let a gal like that get away."

I smiled over to the major. "Roger that, sir. She's the greatest thing since thirty-round magazines. And just for the record, I'm not letting her get away. I'll be home in less than two months, and if the creek don't rise, we'll be married by Christmas."

He cracked a broad grin while lighting a cigar, talking around it as he puffed. "That's great, Yancy. I wish you both the best. Can I take you on out to your camp, or you got somewhere else you need to go?" he said, starting the jeep.

"Well, that's where I'm headed. But you've done plenty already. Hell, you've been up all night, sir. I can catch—"

"Ain't no problem, Brett. I'll drop in and have a cup with Colonel Kahn while I'm there."

As we pulled away from the base-gate guard I asked Wheeler what he knew about upper Eye corps NVA activity around Khe Sanh and Hill 950. I knew the weekly staff briefings he was privy to made him a good source of current intel on the Eye corps battle scenario.

He took a long draw on his cigar before answering. "Well, it really ain't no big secret that Chuck pretty well controls the upper corner of Eye corps all the way from route nine to the DMZ. Heck, ever since the Marines pulled outa Khe Sanh in June of '68 all they can do up there is try and keep a close eye on enemy activity and scrape him with hit-and-miss air strikes when they get the chance. It keeps Chuck honest, but he still rolls through there like he owns the highway . . .''

He glanced at me, tossing a question with it. ''CCN don't run operations in that neck of the woods that I know of. What's your interest in that zone?''

''Just curious . . . I'm going to be hanging my hat on Hill Nine-fifty here in a day or two. I'll be working radio-relay up there during October. A Marine buddy of mine told me they're taking a lot of shit up there.''

''Radio-relay! For who?''

''C and C RTs. We always have recon teams working just across the fence in Laos. And from time to time, we work Ashau Valley targets just south of there.''

''Yeah, I know that, but y'all got those two continuous overflight C-130s in the area. I thought it was their job to monitor your recon teams.''

Wheeler was right. But what he didn't know was that Moonbeam, the night monitor aircraft, couldn't always be raised, communicated with, by a team in trouble. Sunburst, the day monitor AC, was usually easy to raise. But something happened to atmospheric conditions at night, particularly during storms, that made ground-to-air commo sound like you were talking with two cans and a string. When that happened, and the shit was in the fan, a team needed a right-fucking-now radio-relay backup to get air support or an exfil to them.

I knew how critical that need could be. Will and I had been on the odoriferous end of the stick one cold night back in April. Our mission was a BDA, bomb damage assessment, along the Ho Chi Minh trail in northern Laos. We'd moved into a night defensive position during a storm. About midnight we came under heavy enemy probe.

Muffled voices mixed with the ominous crack of

branches told me the NVA were damn close. Using the radio whisper mike, Will tried several times to raise Moonbeam to let them know we were going to move out of our position and might need help. He never made contact.

As I signaled for the team to begin crawling out of our position, Chuck hit us like a swarm of hornets. We blew our claymores and ran, tripped, and stumbled madly toward our alternate rally point. During the frenzied escape I stayed on the radio and finally got commo with some simpleton radio operator in Quang Tri.

The operator said casually, "Well, just how close is the enemy in pursuit?" like he wanted to know the halftime score in a ball game.

I shouted back, "Hang on a second, asshole! I can almost read his name tag!"

Twenty minutes later I raised a Marine relay operator on Hill 861. He saved our ass by calling in some well-placed artillery on the NVA. That was when I'd first learned the importance of radio-relay.

Wheeler slammed on the brakes and swerved to avoid a little girl who suddenly darted into our path.

Looking over at him, I noticed the cigar had fallen from his mouth.

I grinned. "You dropped your cigar, sir."

"I was through with it anyway!" he said quickly, picking it up and flipping it away. He accelerated, shifting gears and the subject at the same time. "Yancy, since you been askin' 'bout the DMZ area, I'll share something with you that's been buggin' me ever since I heard about it. One night in early January, '68, a Marine patrol zapped five NVA in a rock quarry about four hundred meters west of the end of the runway, there at Khe

Sanh. This was before the big NVA siege started, you understand. You ever hear 'bout this?''

"Negative," I said, turning toward him.

"Well, as it turned out they were all NVA officers. And they were all wearing Marine fatigues, and they were walking around this quarry bold as brass. When the patrol intercepted them and called out a challenge to them in English, they didn't respond. Two of the patrol members later said they saw a woman with the group. Anyhow, after shoutin' another challenge and gettin' no reply, the Marines hosed 'em down. The woman, if it was a woman, escaped. But the weird thing about it all was what they found on the bodies, man. Gold! Fuckin' *gold*!''

My mind clicked as another piece of the Hill 950 puzzle had snapped into place. Then, as quickly as it seemed there was some logic coming to me about it, a silent barrage of questions hammered at me. I remembered Bobby Rodriguez telling me that the NVA body count in that region had been over fifteen thousand during the period from February '67 to April '68.

North Vietnam had sacrificed over fifteen thousand men in fifteen months, just to try and control one little measly corner of South Vietnam, and they were still pounding Hill 950. Why?

They had already made the area too costly for the Marines to stay at Khe Sanh. On February 7, 1968, they overran the Special Forces camp at Long Vei and kicked SF out of the zone. Then they proceeded to rout the village Khe Sanh.

Very obviously, the NVA were as serious as two canines in copulation about that little patch of real estate up there. Could it have anything to do with the particle of information I'd just learned—gold?

I became aware that Earl Wheeler was still talking and I hadn't heard a word. I interrupted him, trying to keep my tone casual. "Excuse me, sir. This gold they found on the NVA bodies. Was it refined gold or nuggets?"

The answer was vital. If the wild theory now running around my mind was going to have any credibility I needed to know.

"How in the fuck do I know? And what difference . . ." He glanced at me abruptly, eyebrows raised, like a light was going on inside him.

Looking quickly back at the road, he replied, "Yancy, if you got some wild hair idea they got a gold mine up there somewhere, forget it! All the gold now mined in Asia comes from Thailand, Burma, or the Philippines . . ." He raised a rigid index finger off the steering wheel.

"Years ago they had a small gold mine down at Bong Miue, but that played out a long time back. You see, I know a little about gold, Yancy. I studied mining engineering at Colorado College before I went into the Army. Trust me. You're barkin' up the wrong tree."

I popped a piece of C-ration chewing gum into my mouth and smiled. "I wonder how they ever discovered gold in California without mining engineers to show them where it was?"

Wheeler laughed out loud, then smiled broadly. "All right, smart ass. I see your point. I'll try and find out if it was fuckin' refined gold or nuggets. I don't know what the hell this has to do with the price of tea in China, but I'll look in to it. You realize you're gonna owe me one for this, Yancy?"

I answered while scribbling my mailing address on a notepad. "Roger, sir, just put it on my bill. Hell, I already owe you two or three favors and I've only known you about a day."

I handed him the note. "You won't be able to get in touch with me here, but send it here and they'll get it to me. I appreciate the effort, sir."

He stuffed the paper into his shirt pocket as we approached the CCN entrance.

He stopped the jeep and waited for the Vietnamese guard to open the wide chain-link and concertina wire barrier. A large arcing sign above the gate read:

WELCOME TO 5TH SPECIAL FORCES GROUP
(AIRBORNE RECON)
COMMAND AND CONTROL NORTH—
REPUBLIC OF VIETNAM
"WE KILL FOR PEACE"
Colonel Ivan Kahn commanding

Below the sign seven enemy skulls dangled from leather cords. The skulls clattered against one another like a macabre wind chime echoing through the morning breeze.

Wheeler leaned forward peering upward from the windshield. "I been lookin' at that sign and them skulls every time I come out here. Man, I only know a little about where y'all's teams go and what they do. But every time I see that sign, I know it must be some kind of bad shit y'all get into."

He looked over at me. "Like Tracy was sayin' at breakfast this morning, 'CCN ventures where the sun don't shine.' "

I didn't look up. I could hear the hollow clacking of dried bones and I knew what the sign said. I'd seen it many times.

Base camp CCN was ten klicks south of Da Nang right off the coast of the China Sea. It was commonly called the "sand pit," and it was just that—wall-to-wall sand with bunkers, barracks, and mortar pits dotting the otherwise flat coastal landscape. No trees, no shrubs, and only a sprig of grass here and there. A large rock mass towered out of the sand off the south side of the camp—Marble Mountain.

I peered beyond the bright tin roofs toward the beach area where my hooch was located. I looked forward to seeing my Montagnards again.

The jeep engine strained to plow through the deep sand as Major Wheeler drove us toward the admin office located in the center of camp. Approaching the office, I could see the squatty rotund silhouette of Sergeant-Major Rufus Twitty standing near the open door.

Most sergeant-majors I'd known were outstanding. They're key vertebrae in the backbone of any army. But Rufus was an exception—a kind of military mutation. He was a paper-pushing, spit-shine, bureaucrat type, who kept himself in the office and out of the field. He'd never seen combat.

Twitty had never liked me, but that quickly evaporated into undisguised contempt after I kicked the living feces out of one of his teletype operators for calling Will Washington a nigger.

Although Johnson, the whip-ee, was only in the hospital four days, Twitty still held a grudge against me. He tried to fuck with me every chance he got, but the chances were rare. Twitty's whip didn't have much snap down in recon company because everyone knew Colonel Ivan Kahn was our only boss. And that's the way we liked it.

As we pulled up in front of the admin building Twitty strutted to the doorway, stopped, and propped his hands on his hips. I grabbed my ruck and walked to the door with Wheeler.

Rufus ignored me and saluted Major Wheeler as if he

were swatting a fly off his eyebrow. "Mornin'." The good sergeant-major never called black officers "sir." He made it a point to refer to them by their rank. "What brings you out here to the boonies, Major?"

Wheeler returned a sharp salute. "I gave Sergeant Yancy a lift. I thought I'd have a cup of coffee with Colonel Kahn while I'm here."

"Ain't here! He's in Saigon—SOG headquarters. Be gone two days. Sorry you came all this way for nothin', Major." Twitty stayed fixed in the doorway like he was trying to block James Meredith from entering Ol' Miss. He glanced at me and looked directly down at my scuffed jungle boots. "Looks like them boots is cryin' for some polish there, Yancy."

A normal soldier, particularly my own sergeant-major, could have at least welcomed me back from the hospital after I'd been wounded, before he started the criticism— but not Twitty. I knew he was trying to embarrass me.

I narrowed my eyes and looked into his fat face. "Thank you, Sergeant-Major. It's good to be back . . ." I glanced down at my boots, then back at him and blinked twice deliberately. "The enemy—I'm assuming you've heard about them—well, they can smell boot polish a mile off. That's why nobody in recon uses it." I shrugged. "It's just another one of those sacrifices we poor, pitiful recon soldiers have to make."

I glanced down at his shiny boots, then looked up and cracked a half grin. "Gosh, I wish I could look as pretty as you." I saluted the major. "Thanks for the lift, sir. And for all your help. I'm going to head on down to my team."

He returned my salute, smiling. "Glad to do it, Brett. I'll send you that info when I get a line on it. Keep your ass down and your tires between the ditches."

As I turned to walk away Twitty's voice squealed, the way it always did when he was excited or pissed off. "Not so fast there, Yancy . . ."

His callous tone immediately reminded me of his favorite joke. I'd overheard him telling it more than once in the camp club. It was about an apathetic sergeant-major who had to inform a young soldier about a fatal car accident his mother and dad had been in while he was in the field. He called the platoon out for a formation and said, "I want everyone with living parents to take one step forward . . . not so fast there, Jones!"

Twitty's squeal continued. "Tomorrow mornin' at oh-six hundred hours you need to have yourself bag and baggage on the chopper pad." He grinned. "You're headin' up to Hill Nine-fifty, soldier. Maybe thirty days up there with them grunt, jarhead Marines will shape—"

Wheeler interrupted Twitty, jamming a finger into the sergeant-major's chest like a stick of dynamite. "For your information, fatso, my brother was killed at Khe Sanh; Twenty-sixth Marines . . ."

The major stopped and turned his head toward me. "Will you excuse us, Sergeant Yancy?"

I nodded. As I turned to walk away Wheeler continued: "If I ever hear you bad-mouthin' Marines again I'll knock you into next week's nightmare. Is that clear, Twitty?"

Twitty's stuttering voice almost choked. "Yes . . . yes, sir. I . . . under . . . I understand. I didn't mean . . ."

I smiled and glanced at my watch while trudging through the sand toward my hooch: 1020 hours.

A shout came from a nearby mortar pit. "Welcome back, Yancy. It's about time you got back to work."

I grinned and shouted. "Just passin' through, Mac. I'm leavin' on the morning stage."

In the distance, beyond the barracks, I saw a lone surfer paddling hard to catch a wave. Swede Jensen rose and turned smoothly into the face of the wave, then leaned his tall, lanky body into an arch, cutting a graceful trail up and down the lofty wall of water.

I stopped for a moment and watched him ride out the wave. Swede was a local legend of sorts. He was the best One-Zero in camp. He'd been wounded twice and was now on his fourth extension. I'd been assigned as his One-One, assistant team leader, when I first hit camp. I'd learned the ropes from the best in the business—somewhere in the process I knew I'd made a lifetime friend.

Although Swede was from Santa Cruz, California, his favorite motto came from a Tennessee boy, Davy Crockett: "First be sure you're right, then go ahead." He even named his rifle after Davy's "Betsy." There was a rough-cut glow about Jensen and you only had to know him about sixty seconds to understand the he'd take on King Kong as long as the situation met the basic criteria of his and Davy's motto.

Approaching the team hooch, I was surprised not to hear the normal music and chatter. All was quiet. I walked up the cement steps and looked inside. Empty.

I stepped inside and looked around. CAR-15s hung above the neatly made bunks. Rucksacks and web gear were in proper position. I moved to the large table in the center of the room and dropped my ruck.

Suddenly Arnold Binkowski's excited voice blurted through the door as he lumbered into the room. "Hey, partner. Welcome home." He grabbed my hand, shaking it and slapping me on the back. Then, he drew his hand away as if he'd touched a hot iron. "Sorry, Brett. I forgot about your wounds."

"Forget it, Ski. I'm fine."

Ski paced quickly to the small makeshift bar at the end of the room and grabbed two cups. He blew the sand out of them as he spoke. "How about a shot of Beam to welcome you back?"

"No thanks, Ski. Where are the Yards?"

"They're down at the ammo dump unloading a truck. They'll be back by chow time."

"Let's go," I said, walking out the door.

"Go? Go where?" Binkowski shouted, hurrying down the steps behind me.

The clean scent of salt air blowing in from the sea flooded my nostrils as I turned to Binkowski. "We're going to help the Yards, partner. You've heard that old saying, 'The family that plays together, stays together.' Well, just insert the word 'team' for family and you'll understand."

"Yeah, I understand. But this isn't play, Brett, it's work!"

"You have to stretch your imagination sometimes, Arnold," I said, plodding forward.

Ski's voice wilted. "Okay. I'll try and stretch it."

During the short trek to the ammo dump I explained to Ski about the simple importance of something called "team integrity." I recalled that even at Fort Bragg, when a team got a detail to go pick up pine cones or some other demeaning job, the entire crew, officers included, pitched in to do the work.

I explained that with the Montagnards, "team integrity" was even more important because of their social status in Vietnam.

The Montagnards, or Dega, as they preferred to be

called, were like our American Indians. They were the native people here, not the Vietnamese. But, like our Indians, they got invaded, pushed around, shit on, and classified as savages in their own country.

The Dega's allegiance was to us. They knew damn well that if the war ended tomorrow and we left, they would be back in the fields picking cotton and toting bales the next day. These brave little Spartans were the best soldiers in this country. They fought, sweated, and died for us—not this war or what it meant to the South Vietnamese. They trusted us. We owed them our loyalty—right on down to helping unload a truck.

As we approached the dump, Ski's smile told me his spirit had improved.

Tuong, standing in the bed of the truck, was the first to see us. He leapt from the truck and ran toward me, shouting, "Sar Brett! Sar Brett, we happy you home. We missing you, Sar Brett."

Lok, Phan, and Rham all hurried around me, all talking at the same time and grabbing my arms. They escorted me to a low sandbagged wall. I felt like a dad surrounded by his children.

"Sit here, Sar Brett," Tuong directed. Tuong, barely sixteen, always worked harder than the others to learn English. As a result he was usually the designated spokesman for the group, unless they were arguing about something. "We having presents for you."

"Hey, gang. It's not my birthday."

"No birthday, okay. It special day. You come home."

One by one they removed four bright rings from their pockets and pushed them over my wrist. I'd seen this type of Montagnard jewelry before. The brass bracelets were intricately etched with various symbols and designs of Dega art.

Tuong smiled and pointed proudly to the bracelets encircling my wrist. "Is special Dega good luck for you when you go field with us again. You like, Sar Brett."

I gleamed back at the dark-eyed, smiling faces huddled around me. They didn't know I'd run my last mission on RT Texas—our team. I decided now was not the time to put a cloud over their happiness. I'd tell them later tonight in the hooch.

I held my arms out and admired the gifts. "Thanks, gang. Now, let's get this damn truck unloaded and I'll buy us all a cold beer."

Tuong quickly turned and trudged toward the truck, shouting, "Get damn truck unload. Have beer."

Chapter 7

The shrill, mounting whine of the chopper's turbine pierced the windy morning darkness. I sat in the right doorway of the UH-1H named "Enola Hetero." I cradled my CAR-15 across my lap as I had done many times. But today, I sat alone.

Within seconds I felt the upward surge of the chopper. The slick rose slowly off the pad, hovered, then surged forward and up to the east. I waved back to my team, gathered near the chopper pad. A gray cloud of sand washed over their huddled silhouettes. They didn't turn away.

Tuong held one hand on his bush hat and raised the other with a rigid thumb toward me while he squinted up into the sandy fog. The loud, whopping thunder from the rotor blade drowned out their voices.

They had all awakened with me at 0500 hours. We had breakfast together in the mess hall without much being said. That was unusual for RT Texas. Generally, whenever we ate together, I had a hard time getting a word in edgewise. That's the way it was with the Montagnards. If they were talking and arguing everything was fine. But when they got quiet I knew something was wrong. Trying to find out exactly what was wrong was the problem. The Yards never liked to complain or question my decisions or judgments. To them, any complaint was like admitting a lack of faith in me.

But this morning I didn't have to rack my brain to determine what was bothering them. They were worried. The slow withdrawal had started the previous night soon after I told them I was going to Hill 950.

Their concern and worry was normal. I felt the same about them. I wouldn't be there to defend them, to listen to their problems, and to answer their questions.

Right before lights out I talked with Binkowski and explained how important it was that he always answer their questions no matter how trivial they seemed to him at the time. I told him never to lie to them. If he didn't know the answer to something, it was better to admit it, promise to find out, then follow through.

For Ski to function well as team leader it was critical that they respect him. I knew the Yards wouldn't let him down as long as he maintained that respect. Throughout the conversation, Ski's serious expression made me feel confident that he understood the rules of recon.

The chopper swung north, paralleling the coast. I shifted my position back into the troop cabin and out of the cold downdraft. As I rolled my sleeves down a voice shouted above the rotor noise.

"You want some çoffee, man?" The stout door gunner leaned away from his M-60 machine gun, poking a Thermos toward me. "Use the cap-cup. I got my own." He raised his large black cup. Bold red letters across the mug read, "When in doubt—pull the fucking trigger. 1st AIR CAV." His faded flight suit told me he wasn't a beginner at this business.

I leaned back against the gray quilted matting of the

interior wall and poured myself half a cup of coffee. Handing the Thermos back to him, I shouted, "Thanks. What's our ETA on Hill Nine-fifty?"

"We're gonna dogleg through Quang Tri, pick up some mail, and refuel. We oughta be at Zulu by nine hundred hours if they ain't socked-in up there."

He pressed the button on his headset. A moment later he shouted back: "Captain says that area is still under heavy fog. It could be noon before we can get in." He smirked. "You ain't in no big hurry to get up there, are you?"

I grinned. "Just as long as they don't start the war without me!"

He flashed a smile, then raised the cup to his lips. As he leaned his head back to gulp the coffee I noticed what looked like large animal teeth threaded on a dog-tag chain around his neck. I leaned closer to get a better look.

"Tiger teeth!" he said proudly, pulling the chain from beneath his flight jacket. His hands began to move enthusiastically, like he was about to tell me a fish story.

"We caught this big tiger in an open area near Khe Sanh. Man, I filled that cat full of seven-six-two. Shit, it took all three of us to load 'im in the chopper. I figure he weighed around four hundred pounds. But probably twenty-five pounds of that was lead from this little jewel . . ." He patted his M-60.

"Anyhow, these are some of the teeth I cut out of 'im. Man, do you believe the size of them chompers?" he said, shaking the cord.

I'd heard the ominous night growls of tigers in the jungles of Laos, but this was the first evidence I'd seen of one. The jagged molars were the size of lug nuts.

• • •

At 0720 hours our chopper turned, made a wide sweep out over the sea, then began rapid descent toward the northern city of Quang Tri.

The morning sun sparkled over the dark jade expanse of the South China Sea as we flew over the masses of sampans and boats dotting the coastline. Old men waved from their boats to signify friendship—and to prevent any lethal notions that they might be enemy. The gunner watched them closely.

I glanced northward. Dark clouds massed like bundles of black cotton. Slowly the slick descended into a swirling veil of dirt and landed near a sandbagged fortification.

As the whine of the chopper turbine faded, the door gunner pulled his helmet off and ran his fingers through thick dark hair. He jammed his right hand toward me. "I'm Skip. Skip Period."

I laughed while accepting his handshake. "I'm Yancy. Brett Yancy. Your middle initial isn't 'A' is it?"

"Naw, but I catch a lotta flak about my name. In fact, I make it a point never to even tell a girl my whole name until after I've gone to bed with her."

He jumped out and looked north toward the dark sky, then back to me. "Looks like we're gonna be here for a couple of hours. Once I get the mail loaded, I'm gonna bum a ride down to the Navy exchange. You wanna come along?"

"Roger that. And we need to find the Navy supply depot while we're here." I hopped out, slipped my rifle carrying strap over my neck, then reached back into a side pouch on my ruck and withdrew a silk flag.

"What's that?" Skip asked, looking at the wadded blue and red silk in my hand.

"NVA underwear." I unfolded the flag to reveal the gold-colored star sewn across the face.

"Well I'll be damned! Where'd you get—hey, I'll trade you some tiger teeth for that."

"Sorry, buddy." I tucked the flag into my side pocket. Walking toward the mail hooch, I explained to Skip that I had other plans for Uncle Ho's banner.

Twenty minutes later we'd located the main naval supply depot. It amounted to a long row of six drab Quonset huts. A few questions later Skip and I ambled into the dingy office of Chief Petty Officer Rusty Phelps.

The heavy, bearded man didn't look up from his concentrated assessment of the new Playmate centerfold, open on the desk in front of him. A large sign on his desk read: "If you want it, we ain't got it—come back next week!!!" An index card suspended from the sign by a piece of masking tape added, "If you're Army don't bother coming back at all!"

Suddenly his gruff voice exploded: "I smell Army in here! You gents must be lost." His gaze stayed fixed on the magazine.

I ignored his polite greeting and leaned over the desk to glance at the nude photo.

"Chief," I said casually, "do you know what they call a hula-hoop with a nail in it?"

He blinked, then eased back slowly in the chair and cast a deep-furrowed frown up at me. His bloodshot eyes studied my beret first, then my face. He answered while stroking his tangled beard. "Can't say I do."

I smiled. "An Italian naval destroyer!"

A twinkle flashed through his eyes a split second before a smile betrayed his hard-faced facade. "Italian naval destroyer. That's good."

He carefully folded Miss September back into the magazine and closed it as if he was putting her to bed. He looked up and frowned again. "Now I know you gents ain't here to brighten up my day with jokes. So, how 'bout telling me what the fuck you want? Then, I can tell you we ain't fuckin' got it, and then I can get the fuck back to readin' my latest status report, which you have so rudely interrupted!'' He lightly patted the *Playboy* magazine.

I glanced over to the silent face on Skip Period, then looked back at Rusty. ''Chief, in about an hour I'm leaving to spend a month of R and R with the Marines up on Firebase Zulu. You've probably heard of Hill Nine-fifty.'' I slowed my words while simultaneously pulling the NVA flag out of my pocket.

''I've been noticing for the past few months at every naval station from here to Saigon, that all the Navy gate guards seem to have thirty-round magazines in their rifles.'' I slowly unfolded the flag in front of him.

''Now, I know war is hell on a Navy gate guard. But, I also know there's about twenty Marines up where I'm headed that would think the world of you if you could find it in your heart to loan us a case of those precious items. Thirty-round magazines are about as scarce as virgins on Tudo Street.

''I feel like I could part with this NVA battle banner if I ran into one altruist''—his frown told me I'd used a word he wasn't programmed with—''samaritan''—his face lighted up and I knew I'd hit paydirt—''who could help me out of this problem.''

He studied the flag for a minute, then went back to beard stroking. He smirked. ''Shit, they sell those flags downtown. That ain't no real—''

''Look closer, Chief,'' I said, handing him the silk banner. ''See those bullet holes? That's American five-five-six, sent with love from this very CAR-15.'' I touched my rifle. ''And check the blood on the lower edge. That's genuine NVA blood from an involuntary donor in northern Laos.''

The truth was, the blood came from a water buffalo, but I didn't want to spoil the chief's enjoyment. He was beginning to light up like a kid on Christmas morning.

As he started to hand the flag back to me I sensed the deal needed a little sweetening. I glanced at Skip and winked. ''Hell, Chief, we'll even throw in some tiger teeth!''

Skip drew a quick protective hand to his neck. ''Now wait a fuckin' minute, Brett! You're not givin' my—''

''It's for the war, Skip. You've got more of those, surely.''

''No I don't, dammit! I gave 'em away to the whores downtown.''

Forty-five minutes, one NVA flag, and four tiger teeth later, we were back at the chopper with a brand-new case of thirty-round magazines. Skip was still a little pissed about me giving away four of his last five tiger teeth, but I was confident he'd get over it once he realized the true merit of his sacrifice.

I explained to him it was a matter of fundamentals and priorities. The Marines were always the last to get anything new, and usually among the first to need it.

The NVA had been issued thirty-round mags from day one; they were standard with an AK. But it took our weapons engineers almost eight years to design and build a comparable magazine, and even now, they were in short supply.

I'd managed to scrounge up six of them for my team in a similar trading contest at the Da Nang naval depot some months back. Hard-earned personal experience had taught me that in a sudden contact firefight, the difference between twenty rounds and thirty rounds could be fatal. And even with all other things being equal, in magazine capacity, the NVA still had one big advantage.

The cyclic rate of fire of the AK-47 on full automatic was about half that of our M16. Simply put, in a running gun battle we'd have to change magazines twice as often as the enemy.

The case of magazines I had stowed in the chopper held twenty-four. That equaled roughly one per man on Zulu. When that was expended, it was back to twenty-round mags. I wasn't sure if all this would make any difference when Chuck came calling, but if it saved one man's life, it would be worth it.

As the chopper revved to head north, I said to Skip, "I owe you a beer for this, buddy."

He grinned. "Beer? Shit! You owe me a fuckin' quart of Jack."

Chapter 8

"Five minutes!" Skip Period raised his hand, fingers spread, then turned and swung the M-60 muzzle down toward the dark jungle. The collar of his flight suit quivered in the wind draft like small wings. His squinted eyes searched the moving terrain beneath us for signs of enemy.

I chambered a round and edged closer to the open troop door to watch our approach into the mountainous area. Our cruise speed dropped as the chopper made a slow, wide circling pattern around the twin summits of Hill 950 and Hill 1015.

In the southern distance I could see the awing desolation of Khe Sanh. Bomb craters, jagged trench lines, and decayed bunkers blotched the raw, red landscape that had once been the perilous home of the 26th Marines. Now, it was a war zone ghost town, an empty monument to the men who fought and died there during the fierce rocket and mortar siege of 1968.

I grabbed the binoculars from my ruck and quickly focused for a better view of Vietnam's death valley. My gaze traveled westward along the Khe Sanh air strip until I reached the end.

I searched beyond the runway to locate the mysterious rock quarry Earl Wheeler had told me about. There it was—a lumped, gray crag descending into the shadowy edge of jungle. This was the dying place of five NVA officers, masquerading as Marines and looking for precious gold.

Within seconds my view disappeared. The chopper turned back north. Warm air rushed over me as we dropped. I tucked the field glasses away, looked downward, and got my first view of the rugged slopes surrounding Firebase Zulu.

Rusty hoops of concertina crisscrossed with tanglefoot wire girdled the steep terrain below the sandbagged walls. The crest of the small hill was dominated by a steel-slatted helo-pad. Radio antennas swayed in the dirty wind below us like the remnants of spears on a desolated battlefield. Below the southern edge of the hill there was a garbage heap.

A flak-jacketed Marine standing at the far end of the landing pad tossed a smoke grenade onto the steel surface. Purple smoke billowed from the canister.

As we descended I could see a small, badly frayed American flag dancing in the windy purple haze. The faded banner was tied to the top of a long radio antenna.

Skip shouted through the rotor noise. "We won't be shutting down! We'll be here just long enough to get you and the mail off and the other man on."

I raised a thumb to Skip. Three men rushed to the edge of the LZ, then turned and shielded their faces from the gritty waves of swirling dirt and debris.

The acrid sulfur stench of grenade smoke streamed through the troop cabin, burning my eyes. I tucked my bush hat inside my shirt and pulled my cravat over my nose, bandit style, to filter out the smoke and dirt.

I reached for my ruck and the box of magazines. When the struts hit the LZ I jumped out. Several men ran through the smoke and began snatching sacks of mail from inside the chopper.

I raised my hand up to Skip and yelled, "Thanks for the ride and the tiger teeth, amigo."

He grinned. "Don't let your meat loaf, buddy."

"Roger, and you keep the lipstick off your dip-stick."

"You must be my replacement!" A well-muscled arm heaved a rucksack into the troop cabin.

I turned and looked down at the short, stout black man. No name tag. The jump wings on his fatigue shirt told me he was SF.

Pulling the cravat away from my face I shouted, "I guess you're Jacob Ray. My name's Yan—"

"Glad to meet you, Yan! You can call me Ray, Jay, or fiddle-de-do-dah-day! Just don't call me late for this fuckin' chopper ride home!" His wide grin was missing two teeth. He grabbed my hand and shook it like it was a water-pump handle and he was dying of thirst.

He shouted above the continuous engine whine while he jolted my arm up and down. "Yan, this'll be the quickest briefin' you ever had.

"Number one! The radio, batteries, code book, and all that shit, is in the hooch, over there . . ." He released my hand and jabbed his pointed finger toward the end of the LZ. "I got the last sack of rat poison in camp hid up under the radio batteries. You'll need it! Mix it with crumbled C-ration crackers. Them big motherfuckers love it.

"Number two . . . understand that you ain't op-con, operational control, that is, to this dumb-ass lieutenant here! You ain't in his army. And don't let the son of a bitch buffalo you, or he'll get your young ass killed like he's doing most everybody else up here. Number three—''

"Let's go!" Skip's shout interrupted.

"Gotta get, Yan. Keep your ass down, buddy. See ya back in the world." He dove into the troop cabin as the slick's engine revved higher.

A hot blast of exhaust fumes gusted over me. "Wait a minute! What's number three?" I shouted as the slick rose slowly off the pad.

Jacob Ray yelled back while leaning out the door of the ascending chopper. "Oh, yeah . . . Number three! Don't play poker with these motherfuckers. They cheat!"

The warm downdraft swirled a cloudy mass of dirt into the sky as the slick disappeared over the windy edge of the hill.

Jumping down off the pad, I heard a voice near me. "Welcome to Zulu. Zakary's my name. I'm the resident gunny here," he said, walking to my side.

I looked at the wrinkled, bearded face of the slender man holding his hand out to me. A small silver cross hung half-buried in the tangled mass of hair protruding from his open fatigue shirt.

"I'm Brett Yancy," I said, accepting his handshake. I moved the box of magazines under my left arm toward him. "Since I won't be around here for Christmas, here's an early present for you."

"What's this?"

"Thirty-round mags. Thought you might need these."

His eyes widened with a smile. "Well, dip me in Kayro and call me a flapjack! I thought only generals got these things. Thanks, Yancy. Come on, I'll show you where your bungalow is."

Walking toward the west side of the hill, Zak gave me a brief orientation of Zulu.

He pointed toward two outhouses positioned near the south side of the hill. "The shithouse on the left is named Hanna, for Hanoi Hanna. The other one is named Jane, for . . . well, you know about that little commie bitch.

"Over there"—he pointed east—"that's Hill Ten-fifteen. Every now and then Chuck slips a mortar crew in over there and lobs a few rounds on us. We keep a listening post down there in the saddle between us, but usually they don't hear anything till the first rounds cream in here."

The strong noon breeze suddenly shifted, coming from the south to bathe us in the fetid stench from Jane and Hanna. I let out a breath and turned to study the barren summit of Hill 1015. The charred earth was dotted with the broken skeletal remains of burned and bullet-riddled trees. Thirty meters off the hilltop, vegetation flourished like dull green hair skirting a bald head.

Most of the living quarters on Zulu amounted to holes in the ground with three feet of sandbagged wall around the edges of the depressions. The roofs were made of boards with a layer of plastic stretched over them and anchored down with more sandbags.

One hooch stood out from the rest. It looked like a mansion compared to the others. The structure was almost six feet high and about the same length and width. Mortar-round crates filled with dirt were stacked like big wooden bricks to form the walls. A thick layer of sandbags fortified the outside, top and bottom. Black-painted letters on the door read:

RAY'S ALPINE CHALET AND CARD PARLOR

Zak's gruff voice traveled down his pointing arm. "This here's your pad, Yancy. It's about the best piece of real estate up here. Ray built this hobo's marvel.

"That man couldn't play poker worth a shit. But I'll say this for 'im, he damn sure knew how to build a hooch!" The gunny paused and gazed at me. "You play poker, dice maybe?"

"Neither," I said, remembering Ray's warning.

When he opened the door, I noticed the hinges were made out of what looked like thick seat-belt webbing from a C-130.

"Careful going in. There's a two-foot drop."

As I stepped down into the cavernous interior I smelled the musty odor of wet earth mingled with the stale stink of marijuana. I noticed the radio gear just before the closing door engulfed us in darkness. I heard a low, muffled cough.

"Who's there?" I said, stepping toward the sound. Then, something hanging from the ceiling raked across my face like a claw. "What the hell—"

Zak's laugh ignited at the same time his lighter did. He held the Zippo above my face, revealing a long, swaying row of chicken feet suspended from the ceiling by wires.

"That's Jacob's 'good-luck rooster feet,' as he called it. He wrote home and told his wife to send him a dozen of them bony things the day after we got hit by sappers. Said these things bring good luck. I never heard anything like that, but shit, I guess it worked. He got off this fuckin' hill alive."

He snapped his lighter shut and opened the door. A wide ribbon of dusty light stabbed into the dank room.

"That noise you heard was Mole. Mole Mackenzie. He's over there in the corner. How you doin' today, Mole?" We listened for a few seconds to utter silence. "Mole don't say much. Matter of fact, he don't say nothin', these days.''

Squinting, I saw the drab silhouette of a motionless figure hunkered in the corner. A blanket covered his head and shoulders. Crumpled paper and empty C-ration cartons were piled around him like a Saturday night wino's nest.

I tried to put some encouragement in my voice, which wasn't easy considering I felt like I'd just stepped into a damned time warp. ''My name's Yancy. Guess I'm your new roommate, Mole.''

I waited for a reply. Nothing.

Zak stepped up and out the doorway. He rubbed his beard as if he was trying to generate some reasoning for Mole's silence.

''He's been like that for weeks, ever since the last mortar attack. The lieutenant thinks he's playin' possum, trying to get outa the Corps on a section-eight discharge. If he don't shape up pretty soon I'm afraid Madigan is going to boot him out with a dishonorable.

''Sergeant Ray let him stay in here. But if you don't want him here, say so.''

I dropped my ruck to the floor and pulled the rifle sling over my neck. I leaned my CAR-15 against a wall, then looked back up at Zakary standing in the doorway. ''What the hell. He's not bothering me. Let him stay.''

''Have it your way. I gotta go conduct mail call. Thanks for them thirty-round mags. I'll pass 'em out during mail—''

Suddenly a shout came from outside the hooch. ''Gunny! That mail chopper took a hit. He's trying to make it back here!''

I sprinted out the door and ran, following Zakary to a group of Marines gathered near the south perimeter wall.

A man pointed toward the valley below. "There he is. He'll never make it!"

I peered toward the distant chopper flying low over the Khe Sanh valley toward us. Black smoke belched from the tail boom. I turned to a man shouldering a PRC-25 radio. "You got commo with him?"

"Negative. I can't raise him."

Grabbing the handset from him, I quickly reached and switched the radio to the guard frequency. "Enola Hetero, this is Zulu. Over!"

An urgent voice answered, "Zulu, this is Enola. We're hit. Trying to limp back to your location. Stand by. I don't know if we'll—" The voice cut off into crackling static.

"Enola, this is Zulu. I lost you. Over. Enola, this is Zulu. Over." Silence.

I continued the call signs while watching the slick. He'd dropped to near treetop level approximately five thousand meters south of us.

His struts began to snag branches as he skimmed across the jungle canopy. The radio crackled into abrupt life. "Zulu, we're going in! We're—"

Suddenly the ship plummeted, nose-first, into the dark foliage. A bright plume of flames surged up through the trees. The flames quickly dissipated to smoke.

Tossing the handset back to the operator, I frantically dug my compass from my shirt pocket and flipped it open to get an azimuth on the crash location.

"One-six-one degrees, approximately three thousand meters," I muttered to myself, checking the direction again.

Zakary heard me. "Yancy, tell me you ain't thinkin' about going down there. I know how you feel . . . but

. . . but the lieutenant don't allow nobody off this hill without his permission."

I ignored him and ran back to my hooch to retrieve the radio and my rifle. The gunny paced after me, shouting, "Johnson, where is the lieutenant?"

"He's sleepin'."

"Goddammit!" Zakary bellowed as I exited the hooch with my gear. "Dammit, Sarge, I told you the lieutenant don't—"

I stopped abruptly and got face-to-face with him. "You can tell the *trung-'uy* I'm not in his fuckin' army. There're four Americans out there, down and burning. They may all be dead by the time I get to them, but I'm giving them the fuckin' benefit of the doubt. Understand?"

Zakary stepped back and spoke with a solemn voice. "Look, Yancy, this area is crawlin' with NVA. I'd like to send a squad with you, but I only got twenty men here. Eight of 'em are out on patrol and that don't leave me with much if we get hit . . ."

I quickly slipped my arms through the radio-pack straps, shifted it onto my back, and routed the whip antenna over my shoulder.

"I understand, Zak. I'll make a commo check on the guard freq using call sign Red Rider. I gotta move."

He yanked a map from his pocket and handed it to me. "If you have to call in a medevac you'll need this . . . And if you need some artillery support call me with a coordinate." He grinned. "With the right grid, my boys can put a one-oh-five round in Charlie's rice bag."

Chapter 9

Peering south, I saw a smoky haze rising from the crash site into a dark sky. I knew that once I'd moved beneath the thick jungle cover there would be no chance to get a visual on it again. I quickly double-checked the azimuth, then jogged down the east side of the hill toward the spiraled barrier of concertina wire. I'd have to beat feet if I was going to dig my way through three thousand meters of jungle and make it to the chopper with enough daylight left to get a medevac in.

I made a mental check of my web gear. I had fifteen full magazines, four M-26 grenades, one smoke, two canteens of water, and some pen flares. In addition, I had a first-aid pouch with four Syrettes of morphine and one packet of serum albumin. I also had a PRC-25 radio, but I hadn't even checked to see if it was operational.

"Open the gate!" I didn't recognize the voice shouting behind me.

Stopping, I turned and stood face-to-face with the filthiest man I'd ever seen. Then his odor hit me. I stepped back. The front of his fatigue shirt was so thick with foodstains you could dip it in hot water and make a cup of soup. Although he'd had to run to catch up with me, he wasn't breathing hard. A thick, braided band of rat tails circled his neck.

"Who the hell are you?" I asked impatiently.

His soft reply was closer to a whisper. "Cassidy . . . and you can leave off the profanity when you're talking to me. It don't impress me."

I felt my eyes narrow. "Cino Cassidy?" I said in disbelief.

"That's right. Gunny Zak sent me to take care of you!"

I almost laughed. Then I remembered what Bobby Rodriguez had told me about this motley character. For some reason Bobby thought a lot of him. He hadn't informed me that Cassidy's ego needed oxygen. But Rod had said that Cino knew this area well.

I decided to avoid a pissing contest with the one man I thought might have the answers to some questions still kicking around inside me about Hill 950.

"Cassidy, I'm Brett Yancy. We'll be moving fast. Where's your web gear?"

"Don't carry it. Hangs up in the bush. Got everything I need right here in my pockets."

I glanced at the bulging side pockets of his fatigues, then looked at his haystack of black hair. Rodriguez told me Cassidy had been busted from E-4 down to E-3 for insubordination. I didn't have any trouble understanding why. He was filthy, cocky, self-righteous, and had about as much military bearing as a safe dropping out of a seventh-story window.

Turning the radio on, I grabbed the handset and keyed it. "Zulu, this is Red Rider. Commo check, over."

"Red Rider, Zulu. Loud and clear. How me?"

"Roger. Loud and clear. Red Rider out." I clipped

the handset to my web gear. "Well, at least the damn radio works," I muttered to myself.

"What'd you say?"

"Nothing! Where's your bush hat?"

"Don't wear one. It—"

"Yeah, yeah, I know. Hangs up in the bush. Let's move!"

Forty-five minutes later I'd mentally awarded one gold star to Cassidy—he moved through the jungle with the swift, surefooted stealth of a cat. I estimated we'd traversed over fifteen hundred meters without stopping. Very little of the distance had been on trails.

During a brief rest break I sipped water and ate half a candy bar while Cino gnawed on a short black stick. I made the mistake of asking him what it was. He swallowed a big mouthful and said, "Nirvana nutrition."

Rat jerky. I declined his offer to share it with me. He grinned, wiped the black sap off his mouth with the back of his hand, and muttered something that sounded like "You don't know what you're missing."

Based on everything I'd heard about the size and abundance of rats up here it was reasonable to assume that everyone was, to say the least, irritated with them. But after knowing Cino Cassidy for one hour, I decided that it was more likely that he irritated the rats.

A thousand meters and one hour later we'd reached the general proximity of the crash. A strong wind stirred the trees above us. I could smell the faint, charred stink of fuel and plastic, but couldn't see any indications of wreckage.

So far, we hadn't encountered a sign of the enemy. But it was my guess that if they were in the area they'd be waiting with an ambush near the downed chopper.

The NVA were well aware that we always tried to recover wounded or dead as soon as possible.

The one advantage I had right now was that they would be anticipating an aerial rescue team. Cino and I were coming in the back door on foot, and we'd made good time getting here.

I knelt near the base of a teak tree, located our position on the map, and called Zulu.

The response was immediate. "This is Zulu. Over."

"Zulu, this is Red Rider. We're in the crash zone. Grid coordinate follows: Foxtrot-Tango, three-seven-five-six-three-niner. Contact the search and rescue team and tell them to hold up on a search and rescue mission till I give them a green light. Roger? Over."

"Copy, Red Rider. Standing by. Over."

"Negative further. Red Rider out."

My reasoning for keeping SAR out of the area was steeped in hard-earned experience. I'd been on a rescue operation in Laos that lost two choppers and eight men trying to recover a couple of dead bodies. If I could get the crash site located and cleared, it might prevent a repetition of that fatal mission.

Cino was squatting beside me like a silent Montagnard, staring up at the trees. I handed him my compass.

"We're going to split and search this area. Use this and stay on a two-seven-zero azimuth for one hundred meters. I'll use my wrist compass and head out on niner-zero. If you locate the chopper, don't move on it. Return here and link up with me."

I stood and checked my watch: 1510 hours. "Meet me back here by sixteen hundred . . . You do have a watch, don't you?"

"Don't need one," he said, rising slowly. He handed

the compass back to me and began walking away in the opposite direction without saying another word.

I caught him. "Cassidy, you're going the wrong way! Take this compass and head this—"

"Don't need that. The chopper is this way." He nodded forward.

"Look, dammit, I haven't got the fucking time for you to play Daniel Boone out here! We're doing it my way! You copy that!"

He stared back at me, speaking through clenched teeth. "Two things bother me about you, Yancy. Your dependency on profanity to express yourself, and the fact that you can't read a trail." He pointed upward, keeping his eyes leveled on mine. "See that opening in the canopy? Look at the broken branches. The chopper struts snagged that. The wind blowing in my face has a stink of burnt metal. The chopper is seventy meters this way." His arm went from vertical to horizontal like a mechanical lever.

I glanced up at the break in the trees, then noticed the wind scent. Inwardly, I had to admit that he could be right. What pissed me off was that he thought he knew exactly how far it was to the chopper. He didn't even approximate.

"All right," I said, looking at him. "We'll try your direction. And"—I took a deep breath—"I'll try not to cuss anymore around you. I didn't know you were so damn—darn—religious! You lead out."

He took a step, then looked back at me with a half grin. "I'm not really so religious. It just doesn't make sense to me to risk pissing God off when we're crawling around down here dodging bullets."

I watched him move away into the shadows. I still wasn't sure if I liked this self-styled rat eater. But I was sure of one thing—it appeared Cino Cassidy had his defecation in a tight condition.

Sixty-nine and a half meters later, I crept to Cino's side behind a fallen tree. He pointed forward to the blackened ghost of Enola Hetero.

Part of the tail section and rotor blade still hung in the trees thirty feet above the cabin. The cabin sat upright, wedged between two charred trees. The pilot compartment Plexiglas was melted away, but a mass of black limbs obscured a view of the interior. No fire visible. An eerie fume drifted lazily through the tangled mass of branches.

I strained to see any sign of movement in the cabin. I couldn't hear a sound that might indicate survivors. My concentration was broken by a distant roar of monsoon thunder.

"Don't see anyone in the cabin," Cino whispered. "Pilot doors are still closed so nobody's been in or out that way. I'd say Charlie hasn't been here yet."

"Don't be so sure, partner. Chuck could have been here already and booby-trapped those doors."

Cassidy looked over at me like I'd made a point he wasn't ready for. "Possible . . . very possible," he said quietly.

I shifted my arms from the radio backpack, then pulled the map out and located our position. I jotted the grid coordinate on the corner of the map and handed it to Cino, pointing to the grid. I couldn't wait around and second-guess the situation any longer. The ship had been down for over two hours; I had to move in and look for survivors.

"Cover me. I'll go in and check it out. If I get nailed in there you grab that radio and get the hell—heck—out of here. Call for arty if you get in a jam. Roger?"

Cassidy flipped his selector switch to full auto and eased his rifle over the edge of the tree. "Okay. Got ya covered."

I stood and stepped slowly over the tree. Another crack of thunder echoed through the dim jungle. Then, the rain began. A few steps from the chopper I could see the interior had been gutted by fire. A cautious step farther I saw the twisted outline of a charred body lying across the troop cabin floor.

Slipping my rifle sling over my neck, I reached to pull a brittle mass of branches away from the open area near the M-60.

My stunned eyes stared at the bent, macabre figure in front of me. A single tiger tooth lay on the floor next to him, still attached to the small chain around his blackened neck. The jaw gaped as if he'd tried to scream during the final horrid seconds before his flesh melted away.

A chill rippled through me as I pulled myself up into the cabin. I crouched, leaning forward to peer into the cockpit. The dark ghostly figures of the pilots were fused to the seats. A fetid stench cut through the frenzied cloud of mosquitoes.

I knelt by the side of the gunner in the rear and gently yanked the thin chain from his char-crusted neck, whispering, 'I'll make sure this gets home to your family, Skip.'' I dropped the chain into my pocket and brushed the back of my hand over my eyes.

A moment later I exited through the starboard troop door and looked for tracks that might indicate Jacob Ray had escaped. Nothing. The steady drizzle hindered my vision of the surrounding area. I moved slowly around the nose of the chopper and motioned for Cino to join me.

"Ray's missing. The others are dead. We have to recon this area. He could have been thrown from the ship when it came through the trees.''

"Or jumped,'' Cassidy whispered back.

"Maybe . . . I didn't see his rifle or rucksack in there. He could have been coherent, gotten away.''

My gut feeling was that if Ray had escaped the crash inferno, he'd head south toward the open ground of Khe Sanh and try to use a shiny, a sun-reflection mirror, to signal any aircraft flying over. His only other signal option was a pen flare. But most field troops had an aversion to using pen-flare signals because pilots often mistook the red flare glow as an enemy tracer round and responded with an ordnance run on the location. All of a sudden you became the fuckee instead of the rescuee.

The cloud cover ruled out the possibility of a shiny. Since Jacob didn't have a radio he was in a rock-and-hard-spot situation—he'd have to use a flare. At any rate, there was a possibility that Ray was still alive. I wasn't giving up yet.

I took the radio from Cassidy and shifted it onto my back.

"I can carry that if you want me to.''

"Better not, Cino. I'd hate to see you get hung up in the bush!''

After calling Zulu and giving them a situation report, I looked at the map again and plotted a direct southerly azimuth toward Khe Sanh. It was less than five hundred meters to open ground.

As I started to move out, Cino grabbed my shoulder. "Yancy, wait up. Look at this!''

I turned and took a step closer to the chopper. There on the lower edge of the pilot door someone had scribbled a code in the soot layer with his finger. Streaks of water had partially distorted the letters.

I pulled a pen from my pocket and quickly jotted the letters on my palm—JXDALCOWXSBCHMPXSTHXR.

Cassidy gripped my shoulder. "Ray's alive! I don't know what this damn code says, but I know he had to have put it here!"

I yanked my bush hat over my palm to shield it from the rain while I studied the cryptic message.

As Cassidy leaned closer to view the strange assortment of letters, a light clicked on inside me. The Xs were nulls, used to separate the text. I figured the letters J and R at the beginning and end of the message were his initials.

Gazing at my palm, I spoke the message aloud. "Dallas Cowboys, x, Super Bowl Champs, x, south." Jacob Ray was alive and headed south. He'd used the code to let us know it wasn't an NVA decoy message.

Cassidy came unglued with excitement. "That's great, Yancy. You're unfuckin'—I mean unreal, man. Let's go!"

His uncommon display of emotion told me that he and Jacob were good friends. He ran ahead of me through the rainy forest like a kid at an amusement park.

I sprinted to catch him. "Hold up! Let's take it a little slower, partner," I said, grabbing his collar. "No sense in running ourselves into an ambush. We won't do Ray any good dead."

"Roger, Brett. You're right."

I knelt near the base of a tree and called Zulu while Cassidy took a piss. I let them know we had three KIA and told them I was headed in a westerly direction to intercept one survivor. I also requested they get two Hobos on station, loaded for bear, along with an exfil chopper, ASAP.

I requested the A1Es for support because they could carry their weight in ordnance and their slower speed on strafing runs usually resulted in more accuracy.

Cassidy frowned and asked why I'd lied about our intended direction of travel. The reason was simple. The NVA had a habit of monitoring our guard freq. Since I was having to transmit everything back to Zulu in the clear, uncoded, I wasn't taking any chance on tipping our hand. If Chuck was listening, and I hoped he was, he'd be headed off into left field somewhere to play hide and seek by himself.

I didn't have to tell Cassidy the obvious. If Chuck was already in the zone and he'd picked up our trail, we'd be leading him right to the area where I hoped to find Ray. If that happened, we'd have to fight it out—winner take all.

Chapter 10

I took point and set a quick, but cautious, pace. Two hundred meters into our southbound trek the terrain began to level out and the rain subsided to a light drizzle. The double canopy above us prevented me from making any guess about the cloud-base altitude. If they were too low, the air assets wouldn't be able to get in to us.

American pilots had performed some miraculous feats for me in the past. But to expect them to fly a tactical mission in mountainous terrain during heavy cloud cover was like asking Rod Laver to play a shutout tennis match in a blizzard. If the bases stayed above nine hundred feet, the assets might get in—if not, we were on our own.

Cassidy's foul breath hit me a second before his labored whisper. "Yancy, hold up!"

I dropped to one knee as he knelt near me. His dark eyes were serious.

"Look, man, I don't know how to tell you this, but I got this sixth sense feelin' beating me square in the back of my head. Something is on to us, man. I don't know what, but something." His head moved slowly, scanning the shadowy bush.

I made it a habit never to ignore what Will and I called

TIP—tactical intuitive perception. Will had once saved us from a trail junction ambush by not putting his sixth sense on hold.

Cino and I crawled back into a vine thicket and lay prone—waiting, listening. Strong breezes rustled through the dense tree cover. The low, eerie whine of the wind coupled with a thin haze of drizzle made it difficult to see and hear.

Something moved abruptly in the wet cradle of leaves I lay on. It felt like a rope twining beneath me. I rolled slowly to one side, glanced down, and watched a long snake slither away through the tangled vines.

I eased gently back into position and took a deep breath as my eyes caught a sudden glimpse of movement in the area Cino and I had just traversed.

When the crouched figure came a step closer I saw the rimmed edge of a pith helmet and the ominous muzzle of an AK-47. Chuck had arrived.

Cassidy's soft nudge told me he saw him too. The point man was so close now I couldn't risk a whisper to tell Cino to let him pass.

My experience in dealing with NVA tactics had taught me that they usually put a point man ten, sometimes fifteen, meters ahead of the main body. If they were playing by the rules of Uncle Ho-Hoyle today, we needed to let him pass and wait for the main element. Ordinarily, in a recon situation, I'd avoid contact. But they were too close to where I hoped to find Ray. If I let them get there first, Jacob Ray didn't stand a snowball's chance in a cheerleader's crotch.

I glanced at the selector switch on my rifle, then studied the skinny NVA as he moved into my sights. The absence of a backpack meant he was probably part of a four-to-six-man satellite patrol working off a larger unit. His magazine vest looked new.

He was now three meters out, moving slowly past us. Cassidy carefully turned his face toward me with questioning eyes. I moved my head form side to side indicating "do not fire."

The man stopped abruptly just steps beyond us. I could see his trigger finger tense as he sniffed the air. The wind was behind us—I hoped to hell the drizzle cloaked Cino's odor.

The man eased his trigger grip and raised his arm to signal the others forward. I could feel the tense rush of adrenaline mounting. Within seconds, four dripping figures moved into the zone at close intervals.

It's killing time. The wild scream from my oscillating weapon riveted full-auto lead into the forward figures. Cassidy's M16 hammered rapid-fire bursts. The lethal pelts bit into the bodies, jerking them like puppets on a string.

A frenzied death chorus of groans and howls split through the smoky haze as their blood-spattered bodies twisted and wilted to wet earth.

Cassidy jumped to his feet and quickly shouldered his rifle while I kept my sights trained on the still carnage. He fired a single shot into each head. The rounds cracked into the skulls like a jolt of electricity, jarring the corpses with a final spark of false life. I turned, expecting the point to return any second.

Suddenly the fury of full-automatic AK erupted from the shadows. Cassidy dropped. I rolled right, firing a burst into the muzzle flashes.

The point man lunged forward, ramming his rifle barrel into the soft earth. The weapon lodged upright beside his still body.

I crawled frantically to Cassidy, grabbing his collar. "Are you hit? Are you hit?"

He twisted over onto his back, gasping for air. "Negative, I should . . . I should have had him! I'm . . . I'm sorry, man. My rifle jammed!"

I looked at the open chamber on his M16, then jumped to my feet. "Your weapon didn't jam, Cino. You're empty." I yanked two magazines from my ammo pouch, dropped one beside him, and reloaded my CAR.

"Reload, buddy. We gotta move fast!"

Cassidy pushed himself up, leaving his rifle and the magazine on the ground. He leaned forward, hands on knees, while his scowling gaze traveled slowly over the blood-soaked bodies strewn around us.

"We greased, 'em, man! We greased 'em good! They're ours now and it's payback time . . ." He continued to mutter while pulling a long Kaybar knife from beneath his shirt. "I'm takin' what's ours!" he yelled, dropping to his knees beside a corpse. He slashed wildly across the bloody temple and down into the ear.

I lunged forward, grabbing his knife hand, and yanked him over on his back. I dropped a knee sharply into his chest, pinning him to the ground.

"I can't let you do this partner! You're not one of these fuckin' barbarians." I tried to keep my voice steady while restraining his struggle.

He jerked his head forward, shouting, "Have you seen what these pigs do to our dead? Have you? They cut up . . . hands, arms, everything!"

I'd seen it all right—a naked American pilot hanging upside-down above his decapitated head with his severed cock stuffed in his gaping mouth, eyes gouged out.

The gruesome memory raged through me like a blazing wave of napalm. I jammed my knee harder into him, grabbing a fistful of his shirt.

"You're goddamn right I've seen it! Up fuckin' close! But I'm not one of those scum-suckin' pigs, and I'm not letting you become one. Now get the fuck up!" I released him and stood.

Cassidy drove his Kaybar hilt-deep into the ground. He stood and fumbled to reload his rifle while blinking at me as though he'd just come out of a trance.

"I'm ready," he said, slamming a fresh load into the magazine well. "Let's go."

Reaching down, I pulled his knife from the ground and wiped the dirt off with my fingers. I passed it to him handle first and winked. "Here, this belongs to a Marine. I wouldn't want to see him lose it."

Chapter 11

It was nearing 1730 hours when Cassidy and I crawled slowly out of the bush and into the wet elephant grass on the northern edge of Khe Sanh valley. Strong winds lashed the tall grass. The rain had ceased but low, dark clouds appeared to be priming for another downpour. It was apparent no assets could make it in to us today.

I contacted Zulu and gave them a false coordinate on our location. I wasn't taking any chances on revealing our true vicinity to Chuck. I purposely neglected to tell Zulu we'd killed five NVA, thinking that if Chuck was monitoring my transmission, he'd second-guess our destination based on the ambush location. If I got us zapped out here, I didn't want the word "stupid" stamped on my tombstone.

During the contact Zakary informed me that the weather forecast indicated clear morning skies. But Air Force weather reports were seldom much more than a "definite maybe."

I decided to use the remaining daylight searching for Ray along the treeline. If we couldn't find him by oh-dark-thirty, I'd have to abort the effort and try to get Cino and me exfiled at first light. Although I didn't want to admit it, I knew it was very possible that Sergeant Jacob Ray had already been killed or captured.

I leaned back in the grass and ate the remainder of my candy bar while Cino devoured his last stick of rat jerky.

I decided to conduct a little casual interrogation. "Did you know Sergeant Ray well?" As soon as the words slipped out I realized that I'd inadvertently tossed Ray into the past tense boneyard. I corrected myself before Cassidy answered. "What I mean is, are you friends with him?"

He glanced evasively at me, acting like he was concentrating on the last tasty bite of jerky. He swallowed, then reached over and lifted my canteen to his dark, syrupy lips. When he passed the canteen back I wiped the gummy residue off the opening with my cravat.

Cino picked his teeth with the pointed end of an elephant grass blade as he answered. "No . . . but I guess you could say I sorta know him. I mean, he spent sixty-five days on Zulu. Sure, I talked with him every now and then. Why you askin'?"

The fact that he knew exactly how many days Ray had been on Hill 950 told me there was more to it than he was letting on. I remembered how excited Cino had become when we learned that Jacob was alive. I slipped the canteen back into the pouch and answered.

"Just curious. I didn't know Ray. I thought you might have an idea of what he'd do out here in this situation. Where he might go. You know, friends can sometimes sense that kind of thing in each other."

Cino's eyes widened as he peered into the tall grass.

I pulled the map from my pocket and edged closer to him while pointing to our position. "We're here. You got any hunch where he would go? Would he head this way?'' I slid my finger to the area depicting the abandoned Marine base.

He looked away and began digging mud out of his boot cleats while answering. ''No way. He'd know Charlie would spot him in that open area. Jake wouldn't do that, not in daylight.''

I nodded. ''You're probably right. We'll skirt this section of treeline and search for him. You move east. I'll go west. Meet me back in—''

''No! Won't work. I mean, what if he's injured . . . or wounded. You'll need me to help carry him!''

Cassidy what-ifed me through another half-dozen sentences until I finally allowed him to come with me. Now, there was little doubt that he either knew and cared about Ray or he was a genuine space shot.

I was beginning to think that somewhere between tiger teeth, roosters' feet, and fucking rat jerky, I was developing a few holes in my own net.

As I crawled back toward the treeline with Cassidy trailing close behind, the memory of prudent words from Colonel Ivan Kahn drifted through my mind: ''When you're in Chuck's country, keep your mind on the mission.''

Two hours later a loud clatter of thunder ripped the dark sky wide open, unloading a cold, blinding rain on us. We hadn't found a sign, track, or trace of Jacob Ray.

I didn't like throwing in the towel, but with little light, no chance of air support, and limited firepower, I had no choice. Right now we needed that second basic necessity of life—shelter.

Cassidy crawled to me, shouting through the deluge while pointing south. ''There's an old bunker on this side of the air strip. It's about a hundred yards through the grass. What do you think?''

The stinging pelts of rain on my neck convinced me it wasn't a bad idea. ''Let's go!''

Rodriguez had told me that Cassidy had worked solo throughout this area for several months as an FO before being assigned to 950. Rod was convinced that Cino knew this area better than anyone. I didn't like the idea of spending the night in ghost town Khe Sanh, but it looked like we were going to need scuba gear if we stayed here much longer.

We ran, tripped, and stumbled our way through tall grass, a pitchfork downpour, and mud. By the time I reached the edge of the grass line I'd lost sight of Rat Man.

I waited, peering into the cold pall of rain. I saw the dim outline of a bunker roof. A circular ribbon of concertina wire swayed in the gusting waves of rain like a decayed web protecting the old shelter. The bunker was easily accessible through large breaks in the wire. No sign of Cassidy.

After waiting several minutes I stepped out of the grass into deep water and trudged toward the shelter.

I eased through the wire and approached a narrow covered revetment leading into the bunker. A section of the wall had caved in, forming a knee-deep mound of mud. Boot-sized depressions in the mound told me someone had recently been through it.

Crouching, I edged beneath the dripping overhang into the tunnel. The corridor curved left. I saw a flicker of dim light reflect off the water below a canvas door cloth at the entrance to the bunker. Leveling my rifle, I eased closer and heard the muffled sound of voices—they seemed to be arguing.

"Dammit, I'm lucky to be alive and all you care about is—"

"Hold it!"

Suddenly a rifle-barrel jerked the side of the canvas back. Candlelight reflected across the frowning faces of Jacob Ray and Cino Cassidy. Ray quickly closed the flap on his ruck. I could see a bandage around his forearm.

Cassidy's frown went to a quick forced smile as he lowered his rifle. "Glad to see you made it. For a while I thought I was going to have to go look for you."

He turned to Ray like he was announcing a surprise mystery guest. "Look who I found in here!"

I stooped, moving under a low beam as Cino pulled the door flap back into position. The room was a foot deep in water.

Ray flashed a wide, snaggle-toothed grin. "Yan! It's good to see you. Appreciate you coming after me like you did. Course you know I'd done the same for you, man." He grabbed my hand, shaking it. "Glad to see you got that radio. That's our gate pass outa here!" His strength and quick movements indicated he hadn't sustained any serious injuries during the crash.

I pulled my bush hat off and slapped it against my leg.

"Well, it was a team effort," I said, glancing at Cino, then back to Ray. "I'm sorry the crew didn't make it. That must've been a tough ride dropping through that canopy on fire. You should have taken some of those rooster feet with you."

"Tell me 'bout it. Talk about crash and burn, man! I done been there. Nothin' I could do for the crew, Yan. I was lucky to get myself out."

"My name's Yancy. Not Yan."

"Now that makes more sense. I thought Yan sounded weird, almost Oriental," he said, stepping up out of the water onto a small pile of sandbags. "You hungry, Yancy? I got a can of Cs here . . . beans and franks."

I removed my gear and shifted some sandbags down off the wall to make a place to sit above the water line. As I ate the cold ration the world mosquito population converged on me. I glanced up at the water dripping from the ceiling and saw a big rat scamper along a beam and into a hole. I couldn't help looking to see if Cassidy had noticed it. He hadn't.

He was strangely quiet. I guessed he was trying to maintain the facade that he and Ray weren't friends. But his supposedly accidental discovery of Ray hadn't won any Academy Awards with me. The pinball game bouncing around my mind was flashing "tilt."

I pondered the fragment of argument I'd overheard. Ray's words had sounded defensive. ". . . I'm lucky to be alive and all you care about is . . ." I dismissed my theory that it was brotherly love that motivated Cassidy's excitement during our search for the sergeant.

As the nub of candle began to dim, each of us started moving boards and sandbags around the small cavern to form makeshift platforms to sleep on.

Fortunately, Jacob had a poncho. We stretched it across the ceiling and tied it to the corner supports to keep the dripping water off us.

Ray slapped at his neck. "Man, I'd give a month's pay for some mosquito repellent right now. You got any, Cass?"

"Nope. Don't use it. Got something better," he said, reaching into his pocket. He pulled out a six-inch-long rat tail and began wedging the butt end of it between the sandbag layer like a fuse being inserted into a stick of dynamite. He lit a match and held it to the end of the tail for a moment.

"What the fuck are you doin'?" Jacob asked in disbelief.

The same thought was jabbing me. When the tail began to burn Cino turned to us with a broad smile.

"This'll get rid of the mosquitoes. They don't dig the smell. It'll burn for hours," he announced proudly. "See how it burns? Slow."

Ray looked around the room, gaping. "Well I'll be damned. Cass you oughta write a book: *One Hundred and One Uses for Fuckin' Rats!*"

"You're cussin' too much, Jake!" Cino said with a frown.

As Ray snuffed the candle, the noxious stench of the burning tail permeated the small room. It smelled like scorched hair mingled with smoldering plastic. I coughed, thinking I'd rather put up with the mosquitoes than the stink.

"I'll take first watch, gents," Ray announced. "After that hot roller-coaster ride today I ain't sure I can sleep, anyhow."

"I'm gonna fire up a joint. Anybody want a hit?" Cassidy said, speaking over the soft glow of a match.

"Negative."

"Me neither. That shit'll make your dick go limp, man," Ray chided through the darkness.

Cino replied slowly. "Has just the opposite effect on me, Jake. Makes me as hard as jet-age plastic."

"Now, what good is that gonna do ya? You ain't got no place to put it! Man, you gonna mess around and fall in love with your hand if you ain't careful."

I laughed. "He may be right. You know, between the rat jerky and grass there's no telling what you're doing to your body."

"Yeah, well, this stuff helps me stay in touch with myself."

I'd had friends who started out like that with marijuana—to "stay in touch" with themselves. Months later, they were having to make expensive long-distance calls with heavier stuff.

I stretched back, resting my head on the radio. I thought of checking in with Zulu, but decided there was nothing they needed to know that couldn't wait until morning. I left the radio on, in case they needed to contact us.

For a short time I lay there, fading into sleep, letting the memory of Tracy Gibbs warm me against the chill of the rain.

Just before I drifted off, I heard Jacob Ray say, "Well, I'll say one thing for that Mary Jane, Cino. It sure kills the smell of that fucking rat tail."

Chapter 12

A faint crackling noise stirred my sleep. At first I thought it was the splatter of dripping rain on the poncho above me. I looked at the luminous glow on my watch: 0440 hours.

I raised my head and listened closer. The rain had stopped. The noise cracked again. Pulling the radio handset to my ear, I heard a voice speaking in a whisper.

". . . this is Flight Time. Over. Any station, this is Flight Time. Over."

I keyed the handset. "Flight Time, this is Red Rider. Over."

The whisper responded immediately. "Red Rider, I need some artillery ASAP. We're under heavy probe. Cannot raise base. I say again, cannot raise base. Need arty now. Over."

Questions flooded through my groggy mind. Who were they? What was their location?

"Roger copy, Flight Time. Give me a coordinate. I'll—"

"What's . . . what's goin' on? We hit? We hit?" Ray's startled voice blurted. The sharp, metallic sound of a rifle bolt snapping shut echoed in the darkness.

"Don't shoot, dammit! It's me, Yancy. Who's Flight Time?"

"Flight Time . . . Flight Time," he mumbled. "Oh, that's a Marine recon team call sign. They usually be working along the DMZ . . . What's up?"

"Flight Time, Red Rider. Over."

"This is Flight Time. Go."

"Roger, buddy. I'll try and raise Moonbeam and get some arty in to you. Whip a grid on me. Over."

The whisper came back immediately. "Roger. Stand by one. Grid follows, Foxtrot-Tango, seven-one-niner—"

Suddenly weapons fire resonated in the receiver. Then, his mike unkeyed—silence.

I jumped up. "Flight Time, this is Red Rider."

"We're hit! We're hit! Get us the fuck outa here . . ." The voice continued to yell while intense automatic weapons fire blazed in the background. Again, the radio went silent.

Cassidy struck a match and hurried to light a candle. "What's going on?"

I keyed my mike, shouting, "Blow your claymores! Blow your claymores!"

"Wayne's dead! Wayne's dead! Help us, goddammit!" The voice was hysterical—screaming.

"Blow your claymores, dammit!"

"We don't have fuckin' claymores! Help us . . . please God. Please—"

The empty silence shivered me. My voice cracked. "Flight Time, Red Rider . . . Flight Time, Red Rider. Over."

A moment later a shrill voice spoke as if smiling. "Hey, Joe. How you hang-ee? We fuck-ee you pe-po up number ten-thou, Joe! Ha-ha-ha . . . Wait, Joe. One man still live. I asking him have sum-ting to tell."

I heard an agonized moan in the background noise of chatter.

"Okay, Joe. You lissen . . . him talk."

The dying Marine spoke his last words with courage. "God Bless America and Semper fi! Tell my folks—"

A burst of AK fire resonated through the handset.

"Okay, Joe. Him fini, ha-ha-ha. We having same-same for you and—"

I clicked the radio off and slumped against the wall. A tight-jawed rage shivered through me. Throughout the transmission the Communist pig had purposely kept the radio keyed to prevent me from talking.

Now, I wondered what I would have said if I'd been allowed to talk. Would I have pleaded, begged for his life? Or would I have raged, spewing futile threats of retaliation?

Jacob Ray's arm slipped over my shoulder. "I know where you're at right now, man. Mole and me listened to a team get hit last month. Some of the guys were Mole's buddies.

"A whole team wasted. It's tough when there ain't nothin' you can—"

"How many men on a Marine RT?" I asked, turning abruptly.

Ray shrugged. "About six. Same as a Special Forces team, 'cept Marines only use Americans and we use four indige."

I turned to Cassidy. "They didn't have claymores in their night defense. That's crazy! I've run fourteen missions across the fence, fuckin' knee-deep in NVA, and I never failed to put out claymores in night defense! They saved our ass more than once, when we had to run."

Cassidy remained quiet, staring at the water-covered floor.

I faced Ray, hurling angry words. "Have you ever heard of an SF RT not using mines in defense?"

Ray took a step back. "Look, Yancy . . . I told you I know how you feel. Don't take it out on me!

"What you don't understand is, these dudes ain't SF." He jabbed a pointed finger toward the radio. "They ain't even issued claymores, man! Do you dig what I'm sayin'? They didn't have 'em!"

Jacob leaned back against the sandbag wall. "After Mole's buddies got zapped I asked Madigan why the dudes didn't have any claymores. You know what that silly motherfucker told me? He said recon grunts might face 'em the wrong way, so Marine higher command don't issue them.

"Now, how 'bout that for some flamin' bullshit!"

Ray turned and bowed his head. "I'm gonna make some coffee. Try and get if off your mind. Ain't nothin' you can do 'bout it, man."

He dropped a heat tablet into an empty can, lit it, and set a canteen cup of water over the flame.

I looked over to Cino, then back at Ray. "Sorry I hit you gents, yelling at you like that. It's—"

"Ain't no big deal," Ray said. "Forget it. I'll have some good 'ol army instant coffee here in about two shakes."

I stepped closer to him. "You mentioned that some of Mole's friends were killed in a similar situation. Is that why he's so withdrawn?"

Jake tore the top off a small packet of coffee and spoke while stirring it into the water with his knife. "Naw, man. That ain't why. Don't get me wrong, that episode didn't help his morale none. He'd been like that for days beforehand. You see, Mole's little sister died a few months back. She had muscular dystrophy.

"Mole had always sent all his money home every month to help his family with the medical bills. Anyhow, Madman Madigan wouldn't release Mole to go home to her funeral; said he needed Red Cross confirmation before he'd let him go. Shit, by the time those feet-draggin' turkeys got the word through, she'd been buried a week already. So, Madigan wouldn't let him go."

He took the cup off the flame and set it aside to cool. "Right after that heartache, Mole just crawled up in a corner of my hooch and pulled a blanket over himself. He don't eat much, don't take his malaria pills, and don't talk; 'cept every now and then to Cass, and maybe me sometimes. The rest of the story is, he's got another sister about to die with muscular dystrophy. His family is broke and don't have any insurance on her."

He lifted the cup to his lips, blew lightly, then took a quick sip and passed it to me.

Cassidy stood rubbing a cloth over his rifle. "We figure the reason Madigan won't send him back to the rear is because he's afraid Mole might tell them the story. Jake and me think the LT's hoping Mole will be killed eventually."

Cino's eyes flashed a bitter look as he snapped the bolt shut on his rifle. "But I got bad news for the LT: He'll be dead and zipped up in plastic before that happens! Right, Jake?"

Ray busied himself with heating another cup of water.

Cassidy slapped his palm loudly across the barrel guard. "I said, 'Right, Jake?'"

Jacob kept his eyes fixed on the flame flickering in the can. "Look, Cass, you know as far as I'm concerned that little motherfuckin' lieutenant could catch fire and I wouldn't piss on him to put it out. But you don't need

to be tellin' this man none of our business. You dig?''
Ray's head jerked a nod toward me.

Cino spoke like a salesman handing a pen across the desk to a customer. "Hey, you don't have to worry about Yancy, here. We can trust him. I mean, he came after you, Jake. He's okay. Right, Yancy?''

I took a step toward Jacob. Turning my back to Cassidy, I spoke while warming my hands over the small flame. "You know, Cino, I guess I'm lucky. I've got a boss named Colonel Ivan Kahn who's out-fucking-standing.

"Anyhow, Colonel Kahn has this one-line philosophy he whips on me every time I board the chopper for Laos. 'Remember, keep your mind on the fuckin' mission,' he says." I turned to face Cassidy. "Our mission over here is to undermine the Communists and kick the living feces out of Charlie every fucking chance we get.

"You know, I've heard Colonel Kahn say that fourteen times, now, and I'm glad he does. Because when my mind starts to dull, those words nudge around inside me and help me keep things in perspective." I glanced at Jacob Ray, then looked down at the water about to boil. "I wish that was chili instead of water."

Chapter 13

At 0515 hours I finally raised Moonbeam on an alternate frequency and reported our situation to them. I requested exfil and was told they would do their best to pull us by 0700 hours providing the cloud bases had lifted enough to allow the air assets to get into the valley.

During the transmission I reported the NVA hit on Flight Time. I hadn't received a full coordinate on the team's location, so they couldn't launch a body recovery mission. Eventually, another team would have to go into that area and search for the Marines.

I informed Moonbeam that the absence of claymores in their RON position had been the main reason the team was unable to break contact and escape. I wasn't sure the word would get back to Marine Headquarters in Da Nang, but I was sure that as soon as I returned to CCN Colonel Kahn would know about it. He had a habit of rattling any cage that reeked of command incompetence.

When Cassidy lit another mosquito repellent tail it seemed like a good time to step outside and get some fresh air. I heard whispers as soon as the canvas door flap dropped behind me. I didn't bother to try and listen.

I'd already determined they were in fact friends, that both of them felt an allegiance to Mole, that Madigan wasn't winning any popularity contest, and that somewhere in the twisted scenario they had, at least, plotted to terminate the lieutenant.

I hadn't figured out why Cino wanted to keep his friendship with Ray such a big secret, but I reasoned the plot to kill Madigan, if it was a plot, didn't have much fire left in it considering Ray would be headed home in a few hours.

I'd heard stories about soldiers "fragging" officers that were costing lives with stupid leadership decisions. I didn't agree with the concept. It made about as much sense as a football team flogging the coach if he sent in the wrong play.

I leaned against the retainer wall at the bunker entrance and peered into the darkness. Wind rippled across a pool of water atop a rusty oil drum. Sometime during the night the storm had subsided, leaving a star-studded sky and a crisp wind in its wake. The cool air purged my clouded mind. If the sky remained clear, our chances of being pulled this morning were good. If not, it was back to square one—we'd have to weave our way into the jungle and make it to Hill 950 on foot through Chuck's turf.

Within moments first light began to animate the wind-blown elephant grass. Gradually the dark outline of mist-shrouded mountains came into view. I looked down and found myself standing waist-deep in fog.

A thought hit me as I stared westward—high ground fog is good concealment for movement. I glanced at my watch: 0535. My next contact with Moonbeam was slotted for 0630. If I hurried I had time to conduct a short-range

recon on the fabled rock quarry. I paced quickly back
into the bunker to retrieve my rifle.

"Where you goin'?" Ray asked, watching me hurriedly get into my web gear.

"There's a rock quarry off the west end of the air strip.
I've heard it's one of the sights to see around here! The
weather looks good. We should be out of here this morning. I'll be back in time to contact Moonbeam, so—"

"Wait. Wait a minute, man. I—I wouldn't go down
there if I was you. I mean, that place is rugged. Deep!"

Cassidy's words hurried behind Ray's. "Yeah, man,
he's right. And besides, you ain't gonna see much. That
place is probably thick with fog!"

I was surprised to learn that Cino and Jacob knew so
much about the quarry. I decided to find out just how
much they'd admit to knowing.

"So you've both been down there, is that right?"

They glanced at each other as if wondering who should
answer.

Ray spoke first. "Not me, man. I—I just heard it was
bad. I think it musta been . . . yeah, it was you who told
me 'bout that place, right, Cass?"

Cassidy became nonchalant. "Yeah, probably me. I've
been all over this area when I was working as FO. But
that was a while back."

They both played dumb when I asked if they knew
about the NVA officers killed at the quarry in '68. I
turned to leave, then looked around at their somber faces.
"I'll return in forty-five minutes. I'm leaving the radio
here, but don't contact Zulu. We can't risk anything that
might compromise our position. Roger?"

Ray replied weakly, "Roger."

Crouching, I made my way into the cool, dense fog
and moved west along the old runway. I estimated it was

about sixty meters to the end of it, then another thirty beyond that to the quarry. I knew the fog would make it difficult to see much once I got to the pit. But, if I was able to find any trace of recent activity in the area, it would at least begin to substantiate my wild theory that the NVA wanted this zone for mining purposes.

The torn metal surfacing and water-filled bomb craters in the old runway made it seem like I was negotiating an obstacle course, blindfolded.

Several minutes into the foggy trek I heard a splashing noise, like someone wading through water-filled craters.

I halted and knelt to peer into the haze, toward the noise. The silhouette of a stooped figure moved slowly nearer. My trigger finger tensed.

Finally I could see it was Cassidy. "Cino," I whispered loudly. "Over here. What are you doing out here?"

He crawled toward me. "Jake thought I'd better come along with you. You know, just in case . . ." He turned and gazed into the fog. "Follow me. It's not much farther."

"All right, but keep it low and slow. The last time we did this bit, you lost me!"

Moments later we waded through a stretch of red mud and reached the rocky escarpment of the quarry.

Cassidy looked back, whispering, "Stay close. This gets steep in places."

A chilling breeze swirled over the gray fog like an invisible hand moving over hot ice vapor. As we edged down a narrow, rocky trail I could hear the muffled sound of a dog barking. The deeper we descended the more distinct the barking became.

Cino moved easily along the dim path like a man reading Braille with his feet. It was obvious he knew the trail.

Steps later I could hear the sound of rushing water. It seemed to be rising from the nebulous pit.

I reached to tap Cino's shoulder. "That sounds like a waterfall somewhere."

"That's what it is," he whispered back. "It runs off the Song Ben Hai River, way over there." He pointed into the fog.

The Song Ben Hai was the official geographical barrier, the DMZ, separating North and South Vietnam. I'd seen parts of the river during infiltration overflights into Nickel Steel, North Vietnam, targets. I'd never seen the waterfall Cino was talking about.

The soft approach of morning light began to illuminate the surroundings. Soon, the trail split near a large mass of boulders.

Cino stopped and turned to me. "I told ya you weren't gonna see much down here. We better be—"

"Don't be so sure," I said, taking a step forward onto the other trail. I knelt and ran my hand over the coarse rock. Someone had etched a circle on the surface. A horizontal line had been cut through the center of the circle. "Look at this," I said, touching the stone.

Cino knelt beside me and studied the marker. "Probably some woodcutter's mark. They do that."

Cassidy's evaluation made about as much sense as Egyptian hieroglyphics on an Indian cliff dwelling. I'd seen woodcutter markings in the teak forest of Laos. They always noted their territorial zones with symbols on trees—not rocks.

I stood and strained to see farther down the hazy trail. "Let's check down this way."

"Look, man, I'm tellin' you there's nothing down there but a stream . . ." He looked up into the fog. "I got that feelin' again."

I glanced at my watch. Cassidy's sixth-sense act didn't seem to have the same urgency about it as it had back near the chopper.

"We've got time. Let's move," I said, leading out slowly down the winding path. The rippling melody of the stream became more distinct.

A few steps farther I heard the faint sound of something striking rock. I stopped. A gentle wind carried the noise up the cloudy corridor. It wasn't a ping or clank, but more like a soft clacking sound with no cadence.

I turned to Cassidy, cupped a hand to my ear, and pointed into the thick gray fog beyond us.

Cino leveled his rifle and moved around me toward the noise.

Suddenly a huge antlered head bolted from the fog, ramming Cassidy into me. The jarring impact hurled us back over a pile of boulders. The thunder of hooves striking the rocks rumbled past us.

Cino lay sprawled over me, groaning. I tried to move but was wedged between the rocks with Cassidy's weight pinning me in position. The coarse hairs of his rat-tail necklace stroked across my lips as he struggled to roll off me.

"Are . . . you . . . okay, Yancy?" he said, coughing.

I pulled one arm free and pushed on his back. "I'll be better if you'll get this fucking rat hair out of my mouth! Are you hurt?"

"I got a pain in my chest. Don't feel no blood." He propped his rifle against a rock and pushed away. As he stood, he looked over the mound of rocks separating us from the trail.

"Wow! Did you see the size of that buck, man? He musta been at least ten points, maybe bigger! And that doe with him was huge.'' His labored words rang with an irritating enthusiasm.

I looked up at him in disbelief. We'd just been hurled twenty feet, damn near impaled on a rack of antlers, and Cassidy was raving like an announcer at a livestock auction.

He continued while I tried to get up. "Man, I can't believe the size of—"

"How about skipping the bullshit and givin' me a hand, here!"

"Oh, sure. You okay, partner?" he asked, tugging on my arm.

Standing, I looked around for my hat and located it near the base of what appeared to be a cave opening. Several large rocks had been stacked to cover the entrance. There was a small animal-sized hole near the top of the stacked rocks.

I leaned over the rounded surface of a boulder and peered into the tunnel. "Cino, look at this."

"What's to see? That's just a wild boar hole. They're all over the place here."

Reaching for my hat, I caught a glimpse of something etched on the outer surface of the stone. Looking closer, I saw a circle carved in the stone. I dug the mud away from the small round mark, revealing a rough line chiseled through the center.

I looked up at Cassidy's intense face while pointing to the marker. "How about that?" I said. "There must be a pack of wild boar woodcutters around here!"

Cino ignored my wit. "We better be gettin' back."

Chapter 14

Cassidy stuck to his wild boar cave theory, but I wasn't about to sign any purchase order on it. I wasn't buying his tag-team charade with Jacob Ray either.

The brief rock quarry recon had convinced me of two things: There was definitely some type of clandestine activity being conducted in the area, and Cassidy knew about it.

If Cassidy had discovered a gold mine and was pilfering from it, that would explain why he was trying to prevent me from learning more. The possibility of his taking gold didn't bother me. After all, that was American free enterprise. And the loss couldn't happen to a more deserving enemy, North Vietnam.

What bugged me was if the NVA had a mining operation here sending gold to Hanoi to support their war budget, it had to be stopped. In essence, every ounce of gold that supported and prolonged their war effort was costing American, Korean, Australian, and Vietnamese lives daily.

As we crept from the mouth of the quarry into a thinning veil of fog I pondered the historical connection of gold and war. The discovery of gold in the Black Hills had been the factor that sparked the Indian and settler war. Now, the discovery and elimination of enemy access to gold could be the factor that would speed an end to this war.

"Speculation, Yancy," I whispered to myself. "Pure speculation." It would require a solo night recon in order to confirm or negate my theory—and soon.

The encroaching light made our return trip to the bunker faster but less concealed. Our earlier cloak of fog had quickly burned off to little more than haze. Skies remained clear.

When Cino and I reentered the bunker Jacob Ray was gone. So was the radio, but there was no indication that he'd been captured.

I glanced at my watch. I had less than three minutes until my scheduled contact with Sunburst at 0630, and no damned radio.

"It's cold," Cassidy said, touching the can Ray had used to heat coffee water. "What do you think happened to—"

"Dallas Cowboys . . . is that you motherfuckers in there?"

The soft voice spoke from behind the canvas door flap.

Jerking the canvas back, I stared directly into the muzzle of an M16. I looked up at Jacob Ray's snaggle-toothed grin.

"Super Bowl champs!" I exclaimed.

He moved in, dropped his ruck, and handed me the radio. "Sorry I stepped out, gents. But I wasn't takin' no chances stayin' in here by myself. I was hopin' that was y'all I saw slippin' in here."

I turned to Cassidy. "How about keeping watch outside while I contact Moonbeam?"

"I'll go with you, Cass."

The news from Moonbeam was good. Air assets were already en route from Phu Bai and due on station at 0700 hours. I shifted the radio pack over my back. As I turned to exit the bunker I noticed Jacob's rucksack near the door. I grabbed the shoulder strap and strained to lift it. The heavy pack felt like it was full of anvils.

A hand pulled the door flap back abruptly. "I'll get that, Yancy." Ray's tone was curt as he reached past me and hefted the bulging ruck up onto his shoulder.

I cracked a grin. "What do you have in that, rocks?"

"Ah, yeah . . . how'd you guess? You see, my little girl collects rocks. I promised to bring her some Vietnam rocks. You know how kids are . . . How we doin' on gettin' outa here?"

"Show starts in twenty minutes. We better get outside."

Outside, I peered over the top edge of the bunker. The fog had lifted completely, leaving a clear view of the surrounding area. Cassidy scurried across the bunker roof and lay prone, maintaining a northerly vigil.

I positioned Ray at the south-side retainer wall while I watched the sky for aircraft.

I was hoping for an early arrival of air support when Cassidy suddenly shouldered his rifle into firing position. "Yancy, we got movement over here. There, in that grass we came through."

"Hold up!" I said, raising my head to look across the span of water separating us from the grass. I saw something moving through the windblown bush, but couldn't distinguish any appearance of weapons or uniforms. Then I caught a glimpse of what appeared to be a thick bamboo pole being carried vertically.

I tapped Cino's boot. "Get back down here. That looks like a B-40 team moving in."

Cassidy scurried off the roof and dropped beside me. "You got any binoculars, Brett? I ain't sure that's a—"

"Negative. They're in my ruck back on the hill," I said, turning toward Ray. "Jake, you got any field glasses in your ruck?"

He leaned around the wall. "Naw, man. What's up?"

"We got movement out here. You stay there. I'm—"

Suddenly the earth erupted with a shattering explosion, spewing water, dirt, and debris high into the air. No bunker concussion—they'd missed us. The rocket round had fallen short, hitting the water.

I slammed my CAR-15 over the sandbags, riveting full-auto lead into the smoke toward the grass line. Cassidy opened up with high-volume fire, raining expended brass over my arms. The stench of gunsmoke cut into my nostrils.

Dropping to my knees I reloaded, then felt Ray's leg brush my side as he moved into firing position and began to hammer short bursts.

I jabbed a magazine into my weapon, hit the bolt release, and jumped back to firing position. I expected another round to be headed for us any second.

Our suppressive fire had silenced the rocket team, but I knew it wouldn't be for long.

"Maintain fire!" I shouted, grabbing the radio handset. "Moonbeam, Red Rider!"

A faint voice cracked. "Red Rider, this is Covey leader. I'm inbound. Over."

The call sign told me I had contact with a forward air controller nearby. "Roger, Covey. Be advised, we're taking rocket fire. Need an ordnance run now! Over."

"Copy, Red Rider. I'm three minutes out. Hang in there!"

"Roger, I'm hanging."

I anticipated another rocket or a ground assault any moment. Nothing.

Ray turned his black, sweaty face to me while reloading. "I hope you got something on the fuckin' way. My wife is gonna get pregnant again next week, and I'd like to be there when it happens!"

I leveled my rifle muzzle over the edge of the bunker roof and fired a quick burst.

"Gimme a magazine!" Cassidy yelled.

I reached and yanked two magazines out and passed them to Cino. As he sprang back into position a burst of AK fire ripped across the bunker roof, spitting dirt and shredded sandbag over us. We dropped, hunkering, while another burst riveted above us.

Ray crawled hurriedly to his rucksack and yanked the flap open, shouting, "I got something for that motherfuckin' sniper. I'll French fry his sorry ass with this willy-Pete!" He clutched a large M-79 round in his hand.

"White phosphorous! Where the—what are you going to do with that, throw it at him?" I asked in disbelief.

Ray looked back and winked while reaching deeper into his ruck. He withdrew a sawed-off M-79 grenade launcher.

I gaped at the weapon. The barrel had been cut back about a foot and the stock shortened to fit a hand. It looked like a special Jolly Green Giant–sized derringer.

Jacob quickly broke the barrel open, jammed the round in, and snapped it shut. He crawled back to us and carefully peeked over the bunker roof line, scanning the trees beyond the elephant grass.

He whispered, "Come on, slick. Show me where you be."

I eased near him and rose to eye level, searching the dark foliage.

Two single-shot rounds cut through the windy air. I spotted branches moving. "Two o'clock center, Jake!"

"I see 'em!" he said quietly as he aimed the M-79. He squeezed the trigger. The ominous thump hurled the grenade in a high arc toward the tree.

The well-placed round exploded through the canopy like a Fourth-of-July cherry bomb. The sniper dove wildly from the tree and plummeted into the tall grass.

"Hot-fuckin'-dog!" Jacob yelled, flashing his famous tooth-gapped grin.

"Red Rider, this is Covey. Over."

I glanced upward and saw the small speck of a fixed wing plane in the distance.

"Roger, Covey. Go."

"Looks like we're missing the fun. I saw that white phosphorous burst. Over."

"Roger. How about some nape in that same area?"

"Can do, Boo-boo. Stand by. Have your tickets ready, I got a chopper inbound."

The lead Hobo ordnance aircraft cut a sharp diving turn toward the treeline like a hawk to his prey. A prop drone resonated over the valley as he leveled off at full speed and released the long silver canister hanging beneath the aircraft belly.

The bomb fell end over end and impacted with a roaring wall of flames. The fiery gasoline stink of napalm blistered the cool air as the flyer ascended smoothly out of his bombing run.

"Man, they is some crispy critters in that fuckin' bonfire," Ray said, slapping my back.

The trail A1-E, splotched with dull camo paint, dove wildly through the smoke zone hammering dual 7.62 machine-gun fire into the blazing jungle.

"Red Rider, we're bringing a slick in, pop smoke if you're clear. Over."

"Roger, popping yellow smoke now."

I yanked the steel pin from my smoke grenade and flipped it on top of the bunker. A crisp wind scattered the jaundice cloud over us. The mingled stench of burnt sulfur and napalm watered my eyes. Despite the acrid atmosphere, I felt like I wanted to breathe a sigh of relief, knowing we'd beat the NVA back, but we weren't out of here yet.

"Chopper!" Cassidy said, pointing up into the yellow haze. He scurried atop the bunker and began waving his arms to signal the slick in.

Slowly the whopping thunder of the rotor blades drew nearer. As the downdraft swirled a cloud of dirt and smoke over us, I pulled my brush hat off and looked beyond the retainer wall to see the struts reaching for earth.

I smiled at Jacob Ray. "Nice shooting with that midget cannon, jake. You about ready to exit this tourist trap?"

He nodded while wiping the beads of sweat off his face. "Roger that, Brett. Hey . . . how 'bout you hangin' on to this? Might come in handy someday." He winked and passed the small cannon to me.

I accepted the M-79. "Thanks, Jake. Are you sure you don't want to take this home, hang it over your mantel?"

"Naw, man. I ain't got no mantel."

"Let's go!" Cino yelled, leaping off the bunker.

I pulled the cravat over my face and rushed out into the warm breath of the chopper. It would be a short ride back to Zulu for Cassidy and me. Jacob Ray was headed home at last.

I still didn't know if it was rocks or gold that Jake had in his ruck, but suddenly it didn't really matter. He'd spent sixty-five days in a hell hole. He'd been shit at and hit. He was burned, bruised, and bandaged. As I sat with my legs dangling off the side of the slick, watching the red wet ground fall away from my feet, I told myself: If it's gold he's got in that ruck, he damn sure deserves it.

Chapter 15

The ordnance and FAC aircraft circled Hill 950 while our slick descended into the dank mouth of the firebase. A huddled crowd of cheering Marines could barely be heard above the rotor noise, but their smiles and waving hands sent a hearty welcome to us.

It was apparent they'd been able to watch our exfil fireworks show from a press box perspective peering down on Khe Sanh.

As our chopper struts hit the LZ I knew the good-byes with Jacob Ray would be short—he was headed on to Phu Bai with the slick.

I waited for a moment, giving Cassidy time to say farewell to Ray. I acted as if I wasn't paying attention to his words.

"Stay in touch, Jake. I'll see you when I get home in two months," Cassidy said, patting Jacob's rucksack.

"Yeah, and you take care of Mole. Tell him I said everything's gonna be okay."

Cassidy leapt out of the chopper and hurried across the LZ. I jumped out and turned back to Jacob. He grinned, reaching down to shake my hand, soul-brother style.

He shouted above the whining idle of the chopper, "Yancy, you're one superfine motherfucker. Thanks for what ya done for me, man."

I yelled back. "Like you said, Jake, you would have done the same for me." He quickly pulled a folded piece of paper from his pocket and jammed it in my hand.

"Read this later, buddy. It'll explain some of the shit happenin' 'round here that you don't be understandin' now."

I shoved the paper in my pocket as the chopper engine revved higher. A moment later the slick ascended and Jacob Ray headed home again for the second time in less than twenty-four hours.

I walked toward the small crowd of men waiting at the edge of the LZ. Hands tapped my back as several voices spoke.

"Good job, Sarge . . . out-fucking-standing!"

Zak's voice broke through the others with a tone of amusement. "It's about time you got back here, Yancy. Good show."

I accepted his firm handshake. "Yeah, well, thanks for sending Cino with me. He's a good man in the bush."

"Shit, I didn't send him with you. He volunteered. Couldn't really stop him."

Releasing Zakary's hand, I turned and began walking away toward my hooch. The only think I had on my mind right now was sleep.

"Hang on there, Sarge!"

I stopped and looked back to see a short, skinny lieutenant strutting toward me with a .45-caliber pistol hanging off his hip. His shirt looked like it was still on the coat hanger. The only thing missing was pimples on his face. "So this is Madman Madigan," I said to myself.

He stopped in front of me and propped his hands on

his hips. His eyes looked like two piss holes in a snow-
bank.

"You may think you're some kind of local hero here,
but as long as you're in my command you'd best understand a couple of things. Number one, nobody, but nobody, leaves this fuckin' hill without my permission! The
next thing is—"

I slid my bush hat back on my head. "First thing you
need to understand is that I'm not in your command,
Trung-'uy. I've been here less than a day, seen three
charred Americans, nailed five NVA, and listened to six
Marines die last night. You can stuff your bullshit in
somebody else's face, mister!"

I walked away, leaving him frozen in place.

When I opened the door to my hooch the light streaked
across Mole's face like a trip-flare flash.

He quickly yanked a blanket over his head and curled
into his usual fetal position in the corner. I stepped down
into the musty cavern almost feeling like I should apologize for the intrusion.

I ducked my head to avoid the chicken feet. Then I lit
a candle and found a place to stow my gear. I was tired
and probably could have felt some sense of relief, maybe
even some gratification, if it hadn't been for Madigan's
attempted dos and don'ts lecture. He'd stirred my adrenaline and it bothered me that I'd let a lieutenant piss me
off.

Just as I removed my shirt and sat down on the bunk
I heard a hard knock on the door.

"Come in."

The door opened to reveal the boy wonder of Zulu—
Madigan. He didn't step down into the hooch. I got the
impression that he liked having the height advantage.

"Maybe I was a little tough on you out there, Sarge."

His voice was more diplomatic this time. "But you see, with these jarheads and freaks I'm used to dealing with up here—well, it's the only language they savvy. But I can see that you're a cut above them. I can communicate with you in a way—"

I butted in. "Get this, Lieutenant: I'm not a cut above anybody. For your edification there are two types of soldiers in life: garrison troops and field troops. You haven't realized it yet, but you are in the company of field troops. They may smell bad, but they won't let you down when the going gets tough.

"Now I'm tired." I lay back on the bunk. "How about closing the door on your way out?"

He scowled for a second. After blinking several times he tried to deepen his voice, but it slipped back to an adolescent tone after a couple of words. "Okay, Sergeant Yancy, okay. I can see you have a serious problem with respect. Fine, I'll keep that in mind from now on." He shifted his eyes to the huddled figure in the corner.

"Mackenzie, you better shape up, pronto, or I'll bust your ass lower than whale shit." He smirked. "You know where whale shit is, Mackenzie? On the bottom of the ocean, that's where!"

He glanced back at me as if convinced that the combination of his command assertiveness and wit had impressed me. "We shall meet again, Sergeant Yancy," he said with a smart nod.

"Wouldn't have it any other way, *Trung-'uy*."

He slammed the door.

As I started to snuff the candle out I caught a glimpse of a long piece of paper hanging on the wall near my bunk. The words had been carefully hand-printed. I reached for my flashlight and shinned it across the innovated scroll. Someone had written his own version of the "Desiderata." I smiled while reading over it.

A Marine's Desiderata

Go placidly amid the artillery fire and rocket explosions and remember what peace may be found in body count.

As far as possible be on combative terms with all people.

Speak your truth with firepower and listen for signs of VC and NVA ambushes. Avoid loud and aggressive AK-47 fire, for it is a vexation to staying alive, and you may likely incur a sucking chest wound.

If you compare your M16 with the AK-47 you may become bitter and vain, for always there will be greater and lesser weapons than yours—namely the fucking B-40 rocket.

Enjoy your achievements as well as your plans to kill more.

Keep interested in your survival; however humble, it is the only way you will ever get laid again. Exercise caution in your business affairs for the jungle is full of booby traps, mines, and slanted eyes with vindictive and malicious inclinations toward you. But let this not blind you to what virtue there is and to what tac-air can do. Many people strive for a successful search and destroy mission, but tac-air can make it a reality.

Especially, do not be inhibited about shouting, "Medic!" Neither be cynical about war; remember, it is good for the national economy, and it has given our girl Hollywood Jane a chance to exercise her ambition to become a foreign film star.

Be yourself. No matter what the Corps or the fucking lieutenant want you to be. Avoid altruistic behavior while in the bush and remember that when you got 'em by the balls, their hearts and minds will become very cooperative. Nurture strength of spirit and firepower to shield you on those occasions when the shit hits the fan. Do not distress yourself with imaginings; Charlie wants to rip your ass apart with high-velocity projectiles—and that's no shit. Many fears are born of fatigue and loneliness, but that ain't nothing compared with the fears born in the midst of the mud and the blood and the bullets.

Take kindly the counsel of years (if you live that long) and gracefully surrender the things of youth— but not your hand grenades.

Beyond a wholesome discipline, be gentle with yourself; rough sex was not intended to be conjunctive with masturbation.

You are a Marine of the universe—no less than John Wayne, or napalm, or white phosphorous. Therefore, be at war with whatever the fuck gets in your way. And remember, with all life's sham and drudgery and broken dreams, there are still awards and decorations. Be wild and Semper Fi to be happy.

Grinning, I snuffed the light and stretched back on my sleeping bag.

I awoke to the sound of rain splattering on the plastic-covered roof. I lit the candle and checked my watch. It was nearing 1030 hours. I'd slept for almost three hours and still felt exhausted.

Opening the hooch door, I scanned the sky. The rain wasn't heavy yet, but dark clouds had moved in again. It looked like they could break into a full-fledged storm anytime. I decided to go and make a deposit on Jane's face before the impending downpour began.

When I returned from the outhouse, Mole Mackenzie was sitting up eating a can of C's. He didn't duck back into his cloak, so I figured that either food had the immediate priority or he'd decided to make a public appearance.

His round, unshaven face and short, dark hair, combined with the cross-legged way he was sitting, gave him the look of a Buddha at chow time.

His head remained tilted forward, concentrating on the small can in his hand. The white plastic spoon in his other hand kept an almost mechanical cadence while dipping and shoveling the food from the can to his mouth.

He didn't look up as I moved about and changed into some clean fatigues. But when I took out a spaghetti and meat sauce LRP ration and began mixing some water with it I noticed him look over as if sniffing the air.

When he noticed that I noticed him notice, he went back to digging the spoon into the can again. Soon, the hollow sound of the plastic striking the tin indicated he was near empty.

I spoke while stirring my food. "I got a spaghetti LRP here, if you're still hungry, Mole."

Silence.

I decided I wasn't going to let him ignore me that easy. I leaned toward him. "Here, pass me your can and I'll pour some of this in it. I never could eat a whole LRP by myself."

Filling his can I passed it back to him and began to

eat slowly. He quickly devoured the food, then watched me eat.

After a long silence, I glanced up at the scroll on the wall. "Did you write that?" I kept a look focused on him.

Finally, he spoke. "No. Jake told me a Marine named Adair wrote it. But I know about the Desiderata. Good philosophy."

"How'd you learn about it?"

"My sister gave me a copy for my birthday one year a while back. She said—"

His words stopped. I studied the sad look on his face. Slowly he started to pull the blanket up over his legs.

I recalled Jake's story about Mole losing one of his sisters to muscular dystrophy and decided it was best to change the subject. "You do any writing?"

"No," he said, drawing his knees up to his chest. "Maybe a letter every now and then." He rubbed his nose vigorously with the palm of his hand. "That was good. What you told the lieutenant today about the difference between garrison and field troops. That was real good." He nodded, and for a second, I thought I saw the trace of a grin. Then, he leaned forward with a serious look. "Did . . . Jake come out of that crash okay?"

I had deliberately avoided mentioning Ray to see if Mole would ask about him. Now, the look of concern on his face told me that he and Jacob were indeed good friends.

I answered him and advanced an inquiry at the same time, keeping my voice casual. "Roger. Jake's fine. He went back to Phu Bai with the extract chopper. Cino and I found him down in Khe Sanh. It was Cassidy who located the downed chopper and Ray. Cino seems to know that area very well."

Mole's eyes glistened. "That's great. I prayed for him a lot. And you know what else I did?"

"What?"

He pulled the blanket away and stood pointing up at the chicken feet. "I cut down a pair of his good-luck rooster feet and hid them in the bottom of his rucksack before he left here."

A note of enthusiasm entered his voice. "I did it when he was outside. He didn't even know I did it." He slapped the side of his leg. "Yep, I did it! Of course, I don't believe in that superstitious stuff, I just thought Jake would get a laugh out of it. You know, when he finds them, and well . . . he'll know it was me that did it."

I was glad to see Mole opening up. He was clearly happy and for the moment he had come out of his shell. I didn't know which God Mole was praying to and I had strong doubts about the voodoo magic of cock feet, but if it helped Mackenzie's morale to believe that prayer did it—that was fine with me.

I smiled back at Mole, still trying to find out more about Cassidy. I decided to use the word "we" to make Mole feel like part of the team.

"Well, I guess between God and good luck, we got the job done. But Cassidy was outstanding. He knew exactly where to go down there. Do you know if he goes down there—"

He interrupted emphatically. "Mostly God! That's who did it. I love Jacob like a brother, but he doesn't believe in God! That's his only problem. I've even reasoned with him about it. Like, he believes in evolution. That's incredible! It's insane! I ask you, if this stupid theory of evolution had any credibility about it, then why aren't apes still evolving into humans?"

He didn't wait for an answer. He walked to the door, then looked back at me. "I'm going to take a . . . to pass stool."

A bolt of thunder clattered in the distance as if Mole Mackenzie's God was applauding.

Chapter 16

I was surprised that Mackenzie had snapped out of his depression so fast. I reasoned that he'd reached a saturation point and needed to cast it off or it was just a temporary respite brought on by the good news about his friend's rescue.

My efforts to learn more about Cassidy hadn't worked. Mole seemed reluctant to reveal anything related to Cino. But toward the end of a long, rainy day I had learned a lot more about my roommate.

His actual name was Molnar. His Hungarian mother named him after a famous poet from her country. Mole was an involuntary dropout from Oral Roberts University. He'd been expelled during his sophomore year after the dean caught him in the middle of a heavy-breathing copulation exercise with a shapely coed.

Mole had pleaded with the dean, telling him that God had commanded man to "go forth and procreate," but the dean didn't buy it. He informed Mole that he and his companion had conveniently forgotten about the Lord's husband and wife prerequisite. Shortly after that, Mole joined the Marine Corps and his girlfriend joined the Peace Corps. They hadn't seen each other since.

Although Mackenzie was still chest-deep in confusing religious convictions and beliefs, he was a likable, intelligent guy. He was interesting to talk with as long as I stayed off the subject of God. Where God was concerned Mole was uncompromising.

I found out that it was his religious conviction that prevented him from hating Madigan for not allowing him to attend his sister's funeral. "God teaches forgiveness," Mole said reverently.

Somewhere in the recent trauma of losing his sister and several friends here in 'Nam, he became a kind of "latter-day conscientious objector." And although he'd "changed horses in the middle of the stream," he hadn't bothered to announce it to Zakary or the lieutenant. He was silently demonstrating his new "divine inspiration" by refusing to have anything to do with war and killing.

I wasn't sure if he was fully aware of what was going on inside him, but I understood some of it. I'd seen men go through severe personality changes overnight, after coming off a hot bullets-and-blood mission and losing a comrade. It was a crushing, helpless feeling. When I lost my partner, Will Washington, I wished I could have died in his place.

All things considered, it was my guess that Mackenzie was a short-term trauma victim who still had most of the cards in his deck. I was hoping he would snap out of his conscientious objector routine before he played himself right into a dishonorable discharge. I'd already noticed that both Zakary and Madigan were getting a little thin on patience with him.

The unrelenting drum of hard rain and gusting winds lashed against the hooch door. I reached to tighten the wire-door retainer, then lit a fresh candle.

Along with Mole's revived enthusiasm came an interest in cleaning up his cluttered corner of the hooch. He gathered up the pile of cans and trash he'd been sleeping in and placed it all in an empty sandbag.

I watched him off and on while I studied the signal instructions booklet and the code chart that Ray had left with the radio gear.

After stuffing a piece of plastic into a roof leak, Mole lined up some mortar crates and rolled out his sleeping bag on top of them. Then he removed his shirt and knelt to pray. I glanced at my watch, thinking it was a little early for prayer: 1730 hours.

When he finished, he turned and actually smiled at me. "You want some coffee, Brett?"

"Sounds good," I said, noticing a small crucifix hanging from his neck. "Nice cross. A gift?"

He looked down at it. "Yeah. Cino gave it to me. I'm not Catholic, but it is a symbol of God. You know, Cino believes in the power of the Lord. But—but he just hasn't learned forgiveness yet. He's a bitter—"

Abrupt knocks hammered the door. Mole quickly reached for his blanket.

I opened the door and saw the dripping poncho-clad figure of Zakary. He stepped in and slid the poncho hood back off his head.

He gave me a quick glance, then turned to Mole. "Mackenzie, you got guard duty tonight! East wall, twenty hundred to midnight. You copy that?"

Mole turned away without answering.

I stepped in to diffuse Zak's obvious irritation. "I'll make sure he's there."

"You don't have to get involved in this, Yancy. I'll—"

"I said, I'll make sure he's there, Zak."

"All right . . . all right, Brett. But he's gotta get his shit together and get with the damn program like everybody else around here. The lieutenant's about down to his rope's end with this Marine." He cracked a grin. "And he ain't too wild about you either."

I winked. "That's a real heartbreaker, Zak. You heard anything on a body recovery for the chopper crew?"

"Air Force rescue is supposed to get on it tomorrow if the weather clears again," he said, pulling his hood over his head. "See you later, Brett." He glanced back at Molnar. "Keep a sharp eye out tonight, Mole. You know how Charlie loves to fuck with us in this kind of weather."

At 1955 hours Mole and I stood by the east wall clad in ponchos, peering into the cold windy downpour.

At first, Mackenzie had been determined not to report for guard duty, but I managed to convince him that God didn't necessarily consider guard duty a part of killing. I told him it was more like a responsibility to his comrades than anything else, and since God teaches his children to look out for their fellow man, he was doing the godly thing.

After about fifteen minutes of silence Mole leaned forward on the sandbag wall and spoke without looking over at me. "You better put some rat poison out tonight. This rain'll bring 'em in. I think Jake hid some back behind the radio batteries over in your corner. Mix it with crumbled crackers. They eat it faster that way. Oh, and if you find a dead rat, save it for Cino. He likes rats."

Mole was beginning to reenter a logical state of mind.

The muffled pop of an illumination mortar flare ignited above us, casting a bright yellow light through the haze. The flare drifted slowly across the fog, suspended on the small parachute. I watched it float away toward Hill 1015 like a torch being carried by the wind.

Commonly, lume flares had about a two-minute burning time, but the rain extinguished it in less than thirty seconds. When the light went out, I turned to Mole. "I think I'll go in and mix that poison now. I'll make some coffee for us while I'm at it."

A minute later, as I stepped into the dark room, I heard a high-pitched screech. Something big ran between my feet and out the door. It felt like a small dog brushing past me.

After lighting a candle I noticed a foil-wrapped candy bar lying on a shelf. The rat had eaten most of it, including the tinfoil wrapper.

I located the poison and mixed the red flakes with crackers like Mole had recommended. After placing the mixture in several spots around the room, I dropped a heat tablet into a can, lit it, and set a full canteen cup of water over it.

Gazing at the flame, I thought of Jacob Ray. The note. I'd forgotten to read Jake's note.

I dug through my rucksack to find the fatigues I'd changed out of and withdrew the crumpled paper from the pocket. I held it close to the candle and began to read:

YANCY, THERE IS SOME SHIT GOING DOWN NOW YOU DON'T BE UNDERSTANDING, BUT YOU TRUST ME AND YOU WILL SEE IT WILL BE OKAY. CINO IS A GOOD DUDE, BUT A HOTHEAD AT TIMES. WE BE TRYING TO HELP MOLE, BUT IF CINO KILLS THAT LT IT GOING TO FUCK EVERYTHING UP! IT IS IMPORTANT THAT YOU TRY AND TALK HIM OUTA IT. HE'LL LISTEN TO YOU. TELL HIM THAT PISS-ANT LUTENANT AIN'T WORTH GOIN' TO PRISON FOR! DO WHAT YOU CAN FOR MOLE. TRY TO BE HIS FRIEND. HE NEED THAT. HE IS A GOOD DUDE BUT FUCKED UP AND CONFUSED RIGHT NOW. I WILL BE

SENDING BACK A LETTER IN A FEW WEEKS AND THE
NEWS WILL HELP HIM. YOU WILL SEE.

   CAN'T SAY NO MORE RIGHT NOW XCEPT THAT I APRE-
CHATE EVERYTHING YOU DONE FOR ME, MAN. BURN
THIS. PRESS ON.

Ray had written the note in block letters. He hadn't
signed it. His cryptic tone didn't tell me much except
that he really cared for Mole. I'd already seen Cassidy's
fiery-eyed look of determination back in the bunker. I
knew he was serious about putting Madigan out.

As far as how Jake was going to help Mole, I figured
he probably planned to visit Mackenzie's family when he
got home and perhaps write an encouraging letter back
to him.

I decided not to burn the note. If I was going to give
it a shot at trying to convince Cassidy not to kill the
lieutenant, I'd need Jake's words. I planned on hitting
Cino square in the face with Ray's own undisputable
testimony. I folded the paper and slipped it back into my
ruck.

Suddenly a booming explosion jarred the earth, knocking the candle to the floor. The round had hit near the
hooch. The concussion felt like a four-deuce mortar
round.

I fumbled in the darkness to find my rifle as the hooch
door flung wide open.

"Incoming, Yancy! Incoming!" Mole yelled.

"No shit!" I shouted back, grasping my rifle while
stumbling toward the door.

"We gotta get to our firing positions!"

I grabbed my web gear. "Roger! I'm following you!"

Lume flares popped like firecrackers in the sky as we
scrambled toward a bunker on the southeast corner of

the perimeter. We dove into the cavern jabbing our rifles through the firing ports spraying full-auto bursts down toward the wide saddle separating us from Hill 1015.

A mass of dark figures silhouetted behind glinting muzzle flashes scurried toward our concertina wire zone. The jarring impact of mortar rounds tremored through the bunker like we were gripped in a giant pounding fist.

I yanked a grenade from my pistol belt. I lunged toward the bunker door pulling the pin free and hurling the M-26 high toward the wire-zone assault.

Mole's rifle riveted full auto. Triggered trip flares scattered bright glowing phosphorous light down the wire line, revealing the jagged row of enemy figures rushing toward us.

My grenade boomed, cutting its lethal shrapnel through the concertina into the assault. Black figures dropped away like dominoes.

"Yancy, they're in the wire! They're—"

I'd seen claymores dotting the perimeter but didn't know where the detonation generators were.

"Blow the fuckin' claymores, now! Blow—"

A racketing burst of AK ripped into the sandbagged bunker edge above my head, flushing a gagging shower of dirt over me. I rolled to one side, firing blindly out into the dirt cloud from the bunker entrance, shouting, "Blow the—"

A shattering explosion erupted. Then, another. I recognized the muffled thunder—claymores.

I crawled forward to peer into the smoke and fog. Rain pelted my face as I squinted to search the dying embers of ground-flare light.

Another lume round popped, flooding the perimeter in dull yellow light. Nothing moved. Sporadic rifle shots cracked in the distance.

The sordid landscape was littered with black shadows, motionless bodies lumped amid the rising smoke. Looking through the heavy rain was like trying to see through a moving screen door.

"Medic! Medic!" a voice cried through the shadows. It sounded like Zakary.

I stumbled hurriedly back into the bunker to the web gear I'd left near Mole's firing position. "You okay, Mole?"

Flare light stabbed through the firing port, reflecting off his tense face. "Okay . . . I'm fuckin' okay!"

"Medic!"

I grabbed a first-aid packet off my harness and sprinted out of the bunker to Zak's call.

I located him half-buried in a caved-in trench line. Sliding into the muddy depression, I began digging sandbags and heavy clods of dirt away from his legs.

"Are you hit, Zak?"

He grunted. "Negative . . . But, I think my leg's broken, dammit!"

Two Marines hurried to the edge of the trench and peered down at us. "Gunny Zak. You okay?"

His labored voice growled back. "Yeah, but it looks like I'm gonna be kicking ass with one leg for a while! Don't just stand there! Give Yancy a hand down here!"

We lifted Zakary slowly from the trench. I could tell he was hurting, but he didn't yell out. I pulled a Syrette of morphine from my aid packet and cracked off the plastic cap.

"I'm going to whip a shot of morphine on you, Zak." I jabbed the needle into his thigh.

He grimaced. "We take any casualties?" he asked, looking up at a Marine.

"Negative. Just you, Gunny . . . Oh, and shithouse Jane took a hit. She's a pile of rubble!"

"Couldn't have happened to a nicer shithouse! How 'bout the lieutenant? Did he get hit?"

"Nope, Gunny. Not that I know. But we ain't seen him."

Another man arrived with a stretcher. As we placed Zak on the litter I heard Mole's excited voice shout: "Hey, over here! There's something moving. He's alive!"

I glanced to see Mackenzie standing near a pile of tangled concertina. His rifle was aimed down toward a writhing VC body lying in the wire.

"Hold up!" I glanced at Zakary. "I'll check it out. Y'all get Zak to the medic bunker."

I ran to Mole's position and gazed at the contorted figure caught in the wire. He was moving his head, trying to peer up at us.

Mole was trembling so bad his rifle shook. He kept his wobbling aim pointed down.

"Me no VC. *Chu-hoi, chu-hoi,*" the soft voice pleaded.

There was no weapon near the figure. I touched Mackenzie's shoulder gently. "Take it easy, Mole. Don't shoot. Looks like we got a prisoner here," I said, pulling a flashlight from my side pocket and taking a step closer.

I shined the light directly into the dark eyes of the black-clad VC as I approached him cautiously. He was in a prone position, still mumbling. I knew it was possible he had a pistol or grenade tucked beneath him.

Beads of rain glistened off the face squinting up into my light. "Roll over slowly," I said, searching my mind for the Vietnamese words. *"Lang nga xuong."*

While keeping my light fixed on the figure, I extended

my rifle muzzle into the wire and pushed some of the tangles away.

Slowly the VC turned over onto his back. The dark shirt had been ripped open by the wire.

I moved the light along the muddy body looking for any sign of a weapon. None.

"Hold it, Yancy!" Mole shouted. "Move the light back up some. I thought I saw . . ."

I moved the beam upward along the torso.

"That's—that's a tit! Tit—I mean, he's got titties! Tits, I mean!" Mole stuttered loudly. "He's a girl!"

Chapter 17

"Quiet, calm down," I said, taking a closer look.

Mackenzie was right. He—she—had two prominent breasts. Muddy, but unmistakably female breasts. She'd evidently made it through the wire before the claymore detonation, and had been slammed forward by the back blast from the mine explosion.

She had cuts across her neck and arms, but otherwise appeared to be in one piece. Her hair was cropped short.

"Get up slow . . . *Dung vay cham*," I said, motioning her with my rifle barrel to stand.

As she stood I could see she was young, maybe seventeen. Shyly she pulled the remnants of her torn shirt over her breasts. She bowed while holding the shirt closed with both hands. "I *chu-hoi*. No VC."

Abruptly Cassidy's labored voice blurted behind me. "What you got here? A prisoner?"

Mole's voice stuttered again. "Ti—tits. Tits! He's got tits. Look, Cino."

"Lai day, co," I said, gesturing for her to move forward.

"Well, I'll be . . ." Cino whispered.

"I no VC. No VC," she murmured, shivering.

I stepped forward and lowered my rifle to rest on the sling. I turned my flashlight off, shoved it into my pocket, and knelt, moving my hands over her wet buttocks and legs. "No weapons. Let's get out of this rain. Cino, go tell Zak we got a prisoner. I'm going to clean her up and treat these cuts. You'll find Zak with the medic."

Cassidy smirked. "How 'bout I clean her up and you go tell Zak?"

I looked at him. "Go."

He shrugged. "Just a suggestion. I'll meet you back at your hooch."

Mole and I got back to the hooch with the prisoner a minute before Cassidy jerked the door open. He swooped into the room as if blown in by the monsoon storm. He looked directly at the girl seated on my bunk.

His labored breathing indicated he'd been running. He suddenly slammed his rifle butt angrily against the floor. "Madigan! He's still alive! Wants you to bring the prisoner to his hooch when you finish patchin' her up." He squatted and leaned against the wall, catching his breath.

"Madman wants everybody on line the rest of the night," he said, glancing at Mole.

I noticed the girl's inquisitive eyes widen as Cassidy spoke. She seemed to be staring at his rat-tail necklace.

I didn't like the idea of turning her over to Madigan. Experience handling POWs had taught me to be stern but gentle with prisoners. It was the first phase of good interrogation style.

It was my impression that the lieutenant got most of his military style from old war movies. If he started slapping her around he'd end up alienating a potentially valuable source of information about enemy activity in this area.

I decided to stall Madigan to give me more time to conduct some questioning of my own. "Cino, tell Madigan it's going to be a while. Tell him the prisoner is cut up pretty bad. Roger?"

"Roger. I gotcha, Brett," he said, smirking as if indicating I had other things on my mind. "Come on, Mole. Let's get on line before Madman has something else to bitch about. With a little luck I'll get that prick in my sights tonight and—"

"Hold it, Cino!" I said, standing. "If you got some idea of putting the LT's lights out, get this! You got two months left on this hill and you're home free. You nail Madigan, and at the very least, you're going to prison. I guarantee it. They'll find out who did it. I don't like that asshole any more than you, but killing him isn't the answer."

I jerked Ray's note from my pocket and handed it to him. "Here, read this!"

Cassidy glared at me, then turned the paper toward the candlelight and looked closely at it. As he read the note Mole stepped forward and touched Cassidy's arm. "Brett's right, Cino," he said, sniffing. "And not only that—if you kill him, you'll go to hell when you die.

"You're my friend, I don't want you to go to hell. And, what about my sister? Don't you want to be in heaven with her?"

Cino glanced at the girl, then looked at Mole's sullen face. He reached over and slipped his arm around Mole's shoulder while studying his sad expression.

"Okay, okay. I don't mind going to prison for you, Mole, but I'd hate to have you thinking I was going to hell because of it. Let's get on line, buddy."

He passed the note back to me. "I'll tell Madigan it'll be a while before the prisoner is ready."

When they left I turned to the girl. *"Ten-toi la*, Yancy," I said, pulling a canteen and towel from my ruck. *"Ten, co?"*

She leaned forward and tried to smile. "My name, Lee-lin Hoa. I live Quang Tri."

"Well, Lee-lin, how old are you?"

"Seek-teen."

I was glad she spoke some English. I sat beside her, moistened the towel, and began dabbing the mud and blood off her neck and ears.

I kept my English slow. "Quang Tri. That's a good walk from here. Why you come Khe Sanh? Why you VC?"

Her voice became excited. "Me no VC! No VC! Dae taking me from Quang Tri one year go, Tet. Dae making me work for dem. Dae focking me! Dae number ten-thou! Dae—"

"All right, all right, calm down."

She jerked away from the towel, yelling, "You calming down! You no have focking VC . . . No go hungry, no missing fam-lee—"

"Okay, okay. You no VC. You're a kidnap victim. I un—"

"Me no kid! Me girl. No VC kid!"

I waited for a moment, allowing her to finish the low-level temper tantrum. If she was acting, it was an Academy Award performance.

I'd heard of young Vietnamese being taken by the VC and put through political indoctrination. After a brief crash course in Ho Chi Minh fundamentalist politics, they were given the choice to stay and work for the cause or go back home. The ones that chose home got about three steps that direction and were killed. VC recruiters always made their quota requirements.

I was also aware the NVA often used their surreptitiously acquired soldiers as an unarmed frontal attack barrier to screen the main assault. The fact that Lee-lin had no weapon made her story plausible. It appeared that the only thing dangerous about the girl was her temper.

When she finally calmed down I began applying ointment and a gauze wrap to her neck. A few minutes later I'd bandaged the cuts on her arms.

I pulled an OD T-shirt from my ruck and handed it to her. I placed a towel beside her. "You wash your— chest—and put this on." I gestured to the mud beneath her torn shirt. Then I turned away to give her some privacy.

Her voice softened behind me. "Yon-cee, you wash, please. My arm hurting."

As I turned back to face her, she began removing her shirt. Her breasts jostled and swayed like two large peaches hanging from a windblown tree limb as she moved about, pulling the ragged garment off her shoulders. I helped her pull the shirt off, then placed it aside.

She glanced down at her well-shaped breasts, then looked up and smiled proudly to me. Soft eyes glistened over high cheekbones. A year's hard life in the bush hadn't taken her innocent beauty. She was about the same age as my youngest sister.

"You wash me, Yon-cee," she said again, encouragingly. She moved closer and handed the damp towel to me.

I sensed I was being set up for some close-quarter contact. Her behavior didn't surprise me. It was normal for a girl in her situation to promote intimacy. Intimacy represented a type of security.

I poured some water on the towel and moved it carefully up over her thin shoulders, then down across her breasts and stomach. As my hand moved the wet cloth over her breasts, the dark nipples began to rise. She pressed closer to me.

My conscience nudged me, whispering, "Discipline, Yancy, discipline."

"It feel good for me. It feel good for you, Yon-cee?" she said, slipping her hand over my thigh.

"Uh . . . you know, you're lucky to be alive, Lee."

"I also lucky to meeting nice man who take care of me, making me feel so good." She leaned back on my sleeping bag.

Flickers of candlelight dashed over the contours of her breasts as she spoke again slowly. "I can sleeping here wid you, Yon-cee?"

I reached for the T-shirt and passed it to her. As I stood, she glanced over my body and smiled.

"I hope you liking me. You save me from VC. I like sleep wid you."

"How about putting the T-shirt on before you catch cold. And you might want to take those wet pants off," I said, turning away. "I'll make some coffee and we'll talk. Then, the lieutenant wants to see you."

I noticed the slight hint of a pout on her lips just before she lowered the dark green shirt over her head. I tried to get my thoughts back on pertinent questions as I made coffee.

"Why do the VC want this hill so bad? Many VC die trying to take this hill. Why?" I watched her eyes move from side to side.

"VC no like Marine. Want kill. Dat all I know—"

"No no, Lee-lin. It's not that simple. They're losing a lot of people in this area. Why?"

She stood and walked around in front of me. The long

T-shirt hung to her knees. Ignoring my question, she raised the shirt to remove her pants. She revealed her buttocks as she slid the wet garment down and off.

"I put here, okay?" she said, hanging the dark pants on a nail. The shirt drooped over her hips and thighs. She looked like an olive-drab version of my little sister running around the house in long shirttails. The big difference was that Lee-lin had been torn away from her adolescent years. She'd been thrust into the cruel reality of war.

I still wasn't sure if she was dramatizing an anti-Communist attitude or if she was sincere. But, I was sure that I wasn't going to be the unwitting victim of self-induced naiveté. A good friend of mine had been killed in Kontum by a small boy pretending to sell fruit.

I handed Lee-lin a cup of coffee as she sat on the bunk, then tossed the same question at her again. "Why do the VC want this hill?"

She sipped the coffee, then handed it back to me. "Number ten. No like. You having ha-choc-o?"

"Yeah, I have hot choc-o, but you answer my question first."

She folded her small hands neatly over her lap and looked down at them. Silence.

"Lee-lin, I need to know—"

A sudden rap on the door interrupted me. I opened the door to see Madigan's dripping figure standing in the rain. He was holding a pistol at his side.

He stepped into the room, pointing the gun straight at Lee-lin. She jumped back on the bed, drawing her naked legs up under her.

"Put that away, Madigan! Close the door."

"Is that a wo—woman?" he muttered.

"No, it's a sixteen-year-old girl and you're scaring the

hell out of her! Now, close the door!'' I said, holding my hand to shield the candle from the draft.

He lowered his weapon reluctantly. A wide-eyed look of awe came over his face as he stared at her naked legs.

I stepped behind him and closed the door. He pulled his poncho off and holstered the pistol while trying to recover his command voice. ''So—so, we got us a live VC piglet here,'' he said, glaring down at her.

''She's not hardcore VC. They pulled her out of Quang Tri during Tet—kidnaped. She's—''

He butted in. ''I don't trust anything that can bleed for five days and still live!'' He shook his head briefly and holstered his pistol as if trying to pull his head together. ''Sergeant Zakary has a broken leg and my medic doesn't have any morphine. I'm told you do. Is that right?''

''That's right. I found—''

''Take the morphine over to the medic bunker. That's an order! I'll watch the prisoner.''

I didn't like the idea of leaving Madigan with Lee-lin, but it did have one possible benefit to it. If she had to put up with him for a while, she might become more cooperative about answering my questions. Madigan could piss off the pope without trying, and I needed solid answers while I still had a source of information. I knew that if the weather cleared by morning, there would be a medevac chopper in for Zakary, and the girl would be sent back with it for high-level interrogation.

Looking at her scowling face, I decided leaving her with Madman for a few minutes would definitely be to my advantage.

I took two Syrettes of morphine out of my aid pouch, then looked at boy wonder. ''I'll run these over to the medic. Watch her close, Lieutenant. She may know karate." I grinned.

He stepped back, quickly touching his pistol holster. He looked like a military version of Don Knotts.

After donning my poncho, I left to plod through the downpour toward the medic bunker near the center of camp. Flares illuminated the silhouettes of several Marines moving around the wire zone. They were replacing the Claymore mines we'd detonated earlier. I stopped and squinted through the rain to get a better look at the mines they were setting out. I noticed something wrong— it could be critical.

I jogged onward and down the muddy trench leading to the bunker. A man leaning over Zakary turned and smiled as I entered the dim room. I handed him the Syrettes.

He removed a cap from one, saying, "He's gonna be all right, but this'll sure make him rest easier."

The medic looked down at Zak. "This'll sting for a second, Gunny." He jabbed the needle into Zakary's exposed thigh, squeezed the small tube, then jerked it out.

The gunny's face grimaced, looking up at me. "Thanks, Brett. I hear we got a prisoner."

"Roger . . . Look, Zak, I don't want to tell you how to run your show here, but do your men normally put out claymores without painting the backs of them white?"

"Paint . . . white? Why?" he asked, frowning.

I explained that a common tactic of VC sappers was to slip into a wire zone and turn the mine around facing the inside of the camp. It was always difficult for a guard stationed thirty or forty meters away to see the correct positioning of the mine.

If an attack came and you blew the claymores, suddenly you were hitting your own hand with a fatal hammer.

By painting the back white it was easily identifiable in the correct position. If you didn't see white spots dotting the perimeter you knew something was wrong. I told him that tonight was particularly critical because we already had several large breaks in the wire from the first assault. The poor visibility brought on by the rain would make it even more difficult to spot VC night crawlers.

Zak squinted. "Damn, if that don't make good sense!"

"Do you have any white paint around here anywhere?" I asked, leaning closer to the gunny.

The medic spoke up. "Roger! It's over in the commo hooch. We use it to mark the chopper pad."

Zak said, "Go find Kincaid and tell him to get it handled just like Yancy here said."

I looked at the medic as he jumped to his feet. "Tell him to paint them in the bunker and dry the paint over a candle before putting them out. Otherwise, this rain will wash it off."

"Roger. Be back in a minute, Gunny."

I knelt next to Zak. "Sorry to have to bug you with all that, but it could make a difference on the scoreboard tonight."

"Hey, Brett, I'm glad you told me 'bout it."

I stood. "I better be getting back. I left Madigan with the girl."

"Girl?" he said, moving an elbow to prop himself up.

"Roger, but she's really more like a scared kid."

He blinked several times as he reached for a cigarette. I could tell the drug was taking effect. He spoke as he flipped the top of his Zippo open. "Look, Brett, I've been in the Corps for seventeen years, and I've put up with some screwball officers—NCOs, too. But . . . well, just watch Madigan. His boots don't lace all the way to the top, if you know what I mean. Watch him.''

"Roger, Zak. I figured that out already. You rest. With a little luck, you'll be out of here tomorrow.''

"Don't count on it. Weather update says this storm is gonna be with us for a while. They won't try to put a chopper in here during this stuff.'' He glanced toward the ceiling as a clatter of thunder resounded.

I sloshed and slid through the cold rain toward my hooch. I heard muffled shouts inside as I tried to open the door.

"No! You no—''

"Spread 'em, you fuckin' piglet! I'll split your little pussy in half!''

I wedged my fingers around the door edge and ripped it open. Madigan's naked butt thrashed wildly above Lee-lin. She twisted and struggled as she beat her fist against his chest.

Leaping forward, I grabbed his shirt collar. His punk face winced as I jerked him off the bed and hurled him to the floor. His erection looked like the pride of a stud field mouse.

A gust of wet wind doused the candle as I dropped a knee onto his chest, pinning him to the floor. "Is this any way for an officer and gentleman to behave?'' I shouted into his dark, gasping face.

I stood and pulled his scrawny frame up with me, then shoved him backward, releasing my grip. He bounced off the wall and bent to clutch his pants and pull them up.

His shrill voice stuttered while he fumbled in the dim light. "I—I—was, interro—interrogating the prisoner—''

"What were you interrogating her with, Lieutenant? Your dick?''

"You—you struck me, you. I'll court-martial you, Yancy—Sergeant Yancy!"

I closed the door and lit the candle. Lee-lin was huddled in the corner of the bunk with a blanket drawn up to her chin. I snatched Madigan's poncho off the floor and stepped directly in front of him.

I jabbed the poncho into his hands. "If I'd hit you, your face would be mashed on the back side of your cranium!"

Lowering my voice, I moved my head closer to his. "Do you know the difference between rape and attempted rape, Lieutenant?"

"That's—that's got nothing to do—"

"The difference is, with attempted rape you still go to jail but you didn't get any pussy. Think about it. I count two witnesses here against you. My recommendation is that we forget about this unfortunate episode, and you just chalk it up as a good lesson in self-discipline. Now, what do you think about that, *Trung-'uy*?"

"Uh . . . well, I, uh, guess . . . that—that might be best for all, all con—concerned."

"Roger. Best for all concerned. I couldn't have said it better." I kept a glare fixed on his contorted face.

Stepping away, I opened the door. "I'll guard the prisoner. Good night, Lieutenant."

Chapter 18

Lee-lin Hoa had been raped before. She'd been the victim of several VC assaults on her young body. But the ordeal with Madigan had shaken her a little deeper because of his violent threats. She was genuinely scared. Halfway through a cup of "ha-choc-o," she began to recover.

After replacing a bandage on her arm, I gave her a blanket and my bunk. I set a mortar crate on end and sat on it facing her, sipping my coffee.

I decided that now wasn't the time to press her with questions. I also decided that she deserved an apology from an American for Madigan's behavior.

"Lee-lin, not all Americans are like the *trung-'uy*. I'm sorry you had to endure that. Do you know the English word 'asshole'?"

She nodded shyly.

"Good. Now, do you know the word 'super'?"

She nodded again. "Yes, liking, su-por man."

I grinned. "Right. Well, if you put those two words together, you get what we call a super asshole. That's what the *trung-'uy* is."

She laughed. "We having same-same in Vietnam. You knowing Vietnamese wur for 'ass-ho'?"

"No, I don't."

"Is called '*lo-dit*.' Dis *trung-'uy* is su-por *lo-dit*, yes?"

I smiled. "Roger. That seems to say it very well."

She took a sip from her cup, then looked at me with a slight tilt of her head. "You having wife, Yon-cee?"

"No, Lee-lin, not yet. But in about a month I go home and marry . . . maybe."

"Her name, 'Maybe'?"

"No, no . . . her name is Tracy. I call her Tracer."

"Tra-sur," she repeated. "She lucky girl to having nice han-sum man liking you. Why you call her 'Maybe,' if dat no her name?"

I knew we had to eventually run into some garbled communications. "No, no Lee-lin, 'Maybe' is not a name. It means, well . . . 'uncertain.' You know, like, not for sure."

"Why you no for sure marry Tra-sur? You no love her?"

Suddenly I felt as though I was answering questions like my little sister used to ask when I came home from a date.

"No—I mean—yes. I love her. But, well—"

"I'm under-stan, you thinking she no love you. Yes?"

"No. Yes. Well, sure she loves me. But, you see . . ." I stood, glancing at my watch. "It's almost twenty hundred, aren't you sleepy? You must be tired!"

"No sleepy. Why you no marry Tra-sur?"

I sat back down. "Look, Lee-lin . . . it's this way, you see. People change. This war has changed me. It may change me even more by the time I get home.

"And, well . . . Tracy may change her mind. That's all. Understand? Things change."

She reached forward and touched my arm. "I'm under-stan, but if you love, den love make you understan change. Yes?"

I decided I didn't like being the interrogation-ee. "Okay, Roger, Lee-lin. Now, let's change the subject. Tell me about your family in Quang Tri. How many brothers and sisters do you have? Why do you speak such good English? All that."

After prying Lee-lin off the topic of marriage, I began to learn a little about her recent past. She was from a large family—eight brothers and sisters. Two of her brothers were still serving in the Vietnamese Army as far as she knew.

Prior to her kidnaping, she had worked for the Post Exchange in Quang Tri for two years. It was there that she began to learn English.

During my second cup of coffee I eased the subject back to the present. "Lee-lin, when you saw the man who came in before the lieutenant, you seemed surprised. Have you seen him before?"

"No, I'm no see be-fo. But . . ."

"But, what?"

She looked down into her cup, then raised her head. "A-bou one muth ago I'm hear VC talking a-bou man dae looking for. Is American Marine man dae looking for.

"Dae not knowing I'm hear dem talk. Dae say Marine man having rat tail here." She pointed to her neck.

"Neck . . . the word is neck. The man they want has rat tails around his neck? Is that right?"

"I'm thinking yes. Only hear what VC talk!" she exclaimed.

"Why do they want this man? Did he kill some VC? Is that why they want to kill him?"

Her eyebrows rose. "No, no, dae not wan to kill Marine man. Dae wan taking him POW."

I tried to keep my voice nonchalant. "Huh . . . that's strange. Are there any other Marines they talked about taking POW?"

"No, only man I'm tell you a-bou," she said, looking up as if studying the chicken feet dangling from the ceiling.

She pointed to them, smiling. "Dis is year of chee-kin, nin-tin six-nin. Dat why you having chee-kin feet hang here?"

I glanced upward, then quickly back to her. "No, Lee-lin, those aren't mine. Now, tell me why you think the VC want this Marine—the one with rat tails?"

She shrugged. "I'm don know. You have radio I'm see. You can play roc-a-row mu-sik for me? I'm miss hear roc-a-row.

"I'm like Bee-tal song, call, 'I'm wan ho you han.' You like Bee-tal?"

She seemed determined to stay off the subject of Cassidy, but I wasn't backing down now that I'd learned he had the local VC up in arms and after him.

I leaned closer to the young girl and touched her shoulder. It was time for some gentle inquiring pressure.

I spoke slowly. "Lee-lin, it is very important that I find out why the VC are after Cino—rat man. Is it because he's found a gold mine down in the Khe Sanh area?"

She frowned. "What is gol-my?"

"It's . . . it's a place where they dig, take gold, out of the ground. Like a cave or tunnel."

"No. I'm don think so. No gol in Khe Sanh."

I examined her eyes carefully. I knew it was possible the VC had kept the news of gold a well-guarded secret from the conscript, lower rank, personnel. Her eyes sparkled with sincerity.

She remained silent as if waiting for another question.

"Okay, Lee-lin, okay. I think there is something very valuable, very important, in the Khe Sanh area. If not gold, what?"

She shrugged, then leaned forward to set her cup on the radio table. "I'm don't know. Maybe . . . chee-kin feet!" She giggled, pointing upward.

"Dammit, Lee-lin! Don't play me for a dumb-ass! The NVA and the damn VC have lost over fifteen thousand men kicking the Marines out of Khe Sanh. And they're still losing more people every week trying to take this worthless hill. Not to mention that they want Cassidy as a prisoner! Now, what the hell is up?"

Her frightened eyes glanced involuntarily upward as if taking my question literally.

I lowered my voice. "I don't mean up there, Lee-lin. I mean, why . . . what's going on? Can you tell me anything?"

She sniffed, "I'm can telling you I missing my mamasan and my papasan *beau coup*." She lay back on the bunk and drew her legs up into a fetal position.

I stood slowly, then pulled a blanket over her. "Okay, I'm sorry I yelled at you. You get some rest. It's obvious you don't know much more. And thanks for telling me about Cassidy."

She raised her head with a sleepy smile. "Yon-cee, I'm tee-tee and no take much place here in you bed. You pleasing sleep wid me?"

"No, I'm going to make some coffee for Mole and Cino, then I'll get on line for the rest of the night with them. You sleep."

Her smile dropped when she heard the repetitive rum-

ble of arclight explosions in the distance. I estimated the
explosions were coming from Laos, seven miles west of
us, near the Ho Chi Minh trail.

She gazed toward the continuing low growl of noise as
if she knew, or had heard from the VC, what the high-
altitude bombing missions could do. Perhaps, if the VC
had used her to foot-shuttle material and ammo out of
Laos, she'd seen the terrifying results up close.

After a moment, she pulled the blanket up to her chin
and closed her weary eyes.

As the distant bomb thunder faded I became aware of
the incessant drone of rain pelting the hooch. I dug
through a side pouch of my rucksack, found another
packet of instant coffee, and heated some water.

I thought back to a bomb-damage-assessment mission
Will and I had conducted months ago east of a place
called Ta-ha, Laos. I'd always considered BDAs the
lowest rung on the SOG mission priority ladder. It
seemed ludicrous that we had to go into a heavily occupied enemy area to take pictures of bomb destruction for
some staff jockey at SOG headquarters to drool over.

The B-52 saturation bombing missions rained 500- and
750-pound bombs from an altitude of 20,000 feet. The
resulting devastation was awesome. Twenty-mile spans
of what was once beautiful, dense jungle were suddenly
transformed into a cratered mass of splintered trees and
tangled, dead vegetation.

On the morning we entered the arclighted area it
seemed as though I was walking into a nightmare dimen-
sion. It was quiet, eerie—like mammoth demons had
slashed through, leaving huge footprints in the raped
landscape.

The stale scent of exploded cordite drifted through the
hazy veil of ground fog that morning. Will Washington

took point and led out slowly. Sixty meters into the stinking bomb zone Will stopped and motioned me forward.

"Brett, look up to the left of that pile of trees," he said, handing me the binoculars. "Looks like a graveyard done been dug up!"

Taking the field glasses, I focused on the area. Body parts, arms and legs, were sticking out of a huge mound of earth. It looked as though the entrails of hell had boiled up beneath a cemetery, ripping and strewing the sleeping remains of fresh corpses everywhere.

After signaling for the Montagnards to cover us, Will and I moved forward to get a closer look. I picked up a tree limb to use as a cane as we stumbled through the lumped wreckage of what was once an underground bunker complex.

The complex had been part of a weapons and ammo cache. There had been several secondary detonations triggered by the arclight. The sour odor of death permeated the air.

I pulled the small *Penn-ee* camera from my pocket and began photographing. Then I noticed something strange about the pieces of human remains. Some of the severed arms and legs had bandages on them. One grayish leg had a part of a shattered cast on it.

It appeared that an infirmary had been part of the tunnel network.

"This is all kinda ironic," Will said, pointing out over the human debris.

"What do you mean, partner?"

His dark eyes squinted, looking back at me. "What I'm saying is that this arclight has just proceeded to kill a bunch of people that were probably already dying."

I tucked my camera away and glanced around. "I guess you could call this overkill in the first degree."

During a photo debriefing session back at SOG head-quarters, I learned from a psy-ops officer that arclights had another benefit beyond the obvious ability to pulver-ize enemy concentrations.

He told me that NVA prisoners had revealed the number one thing they feared most in our arsenal was arclights. A prisoner had related that one morning he was eating breakfast with his unit when suddenly a roll-ing thunderous explosion catapulted him through the jungle like a stone. He awoke surrounded by bits and pieces of his dead comrades.

The prisoner said that the absence of a warning sound worked on their morale—like they were always walking beneath an invisible aerial mine field.

I still remembered the smell. I poured the packet of coffee into the water and stirred it. As I left the hooch to go meet Cino and Mole, I glanced toward Lee-lin. She was still curled in the fetal position on my bunk, sound asleep. Again, I thought about my little sister—I was glad Lee-lin hadn't gotten caught by the arclights.

Chapter 19

I left Lee-lin asleep in the hooch and made my way toward the east perimeter bunker that Mole and I had occupied during the attack. I kept my bush hat over the canteen cup of hot coffee as I trudged forward in the wet wind.

Through the rain I could see a clump of broken, shattered wood piled on top of everybody's favorite shithouse—Jane. Hanna had survived the assault.

As I crept into the bunker I saw Cassidy and Mole hunkered near a firing port. They both noticed me enter.

I passed the cup to Mole. "This'll help keep your eyelids peeled for a while. Careful, it's hot."

"Thanks, Brett," Mole said, taking a sip. He passed the cup to Cino.

I twisted my soaked bush hat, wringing the water out, then straightened it and slid my poncho hood back.

I put my hat on and leaned forward to look out the narrow window. "Seen any signs of an encore from Charlie and company?"

"Not yet," Cassidy answered. "What'd you do with the girl? You give her to Madigan?"

"He saw her. She's sleeping now." I avoided telling

them that Madigan's interrogation style meant trying to pump information from her with the wrong instrument.

Mole took another sip of java, then frowned as if he was concentrating on something profound. He spoke while passing the cup over to Cino. "She—she seems like a nice girl. I can't imagine her as a V—VC."

I gave Cassidy and Mole a condensed version of what I'd just learned about Lee-lin. I omitted telling them that she had informed me that Cino was a wanted man. My omission had a purpose to it—I planned to see if Cino would admit to anything about his solo missions into Khe Sanh before I tipped my hand.

Looking out at a fading lume flare I tossed him a question. "Cino, you've been around this area awhile. You've worked as FO along the DMZ. You've seen a lot happening here.

"Why is this area so important? Why does Chuck keep losing people trying to overrun this hill?" I turned to him.

He squatted and took out a rat jerky. He clamped his teeth over it, pulled hard at the black stick, and answered while chewing. "Elementary . . . Watson. This is a primary NVA infiltration route. That's the only reason they want us outa here."

His reasoning seemed more like a clever excuse. I was well aware that route nine, located ten klicks south of us, was a very desirable road for NVA use. It came directly out of Laos and ran due east through Khe Sanh to Quang Tri.

Blasting the Marines out of base Khe Sanh may have helped the NVA secure the road as a variable avenue of night infiltration, but that didn't have anything to do with Hill 950. We couldn't see route nine from here with a telescope—mountains prevented our observation of it.

It was inconceivable that Hill 950 had any tactical advantage to the NVA. And, even if Charlie succeeded in taking Zulu, he knew damn well he couldn't occupy the hill—tac-air would hit him so hard it would blow his ass all the way back to Laos.

After explaining the simple logic of the tactical scenario to Cassidy, he still played dumb.

As I wiped the sap residue off the community coffee cup and took a drink I decided to hit Cino from another angle.

"I met a Marine named Bobby Rodriguez while I was in Ninety-fifth medevac a few days. He said he knew you."

Cino licked the jerky, then stuck it into his pocket. "Yeah, I know Rod. He took a bad hit up here. Lost a leg."

"We were roommates. I really like Bobby. He talked about you some. He thought a lot of you. Said you went out on night solo recons around here."

Cassidy's eyes flashed. He remained silent.

I handed the near-empty cup to Mole, who was looking out the bunker window. "Mole, you want to go in and make us a refill on this? You can check on Lee-lin, while you're at it."

"Okay, Brett. I'll—I'll do that. She's a nice girl. I mean . . . right?"

I nodded reassuringly. "Roger, Mole. She's not VC. I don't think we have anything to worry about but her temper. Just make sure you don't call her a VC or a kid." I winked.

When Mackenzie left I pressed Cassidy again. "Why would you want to conduct night solo recons around here? Did Madigan know about it?"

He stood and walked to the firing port. "No, that anus

don't know . . . nothing. Sure, I'd go out every now and then to check the area. You know, just to make sure we didn't have sappers probing us.''

"I guess that makes sense," I said, moving closer. "Now let me hit you with some elementary news, Watson. I learned from the girl that the local rice burners want you as a prisoner. Got any idea why?''

He laughed. "What? That's bull! They want any American as a prisoner. You know, puts a feather in their cap.''

"Well, it occurred to me that you are possibly the main reason they're putting so much emphasis on this hill. And why wouldn't they just kill you? Do you think they may want your recipe for rat jerky?''

Cassidy spun around, glaring at me. "Look, Yancy, you're pushing a little too hard. How 'bout backin' off the forty questions! You're startin' to—''

Mole's labored voice shouted as he stumbled in. "Brett, Brett! She's, she's gone! The girl, the prisoner, I mean!''

"Dammit! Where's Madigan's hooch?'' I shouted to Mole.

"I, I—don't know where—''

Cino stood and moved past me. "Come on. I'll show you. It's under the north end of the chopper pad.''

"You stay here, Mole.''

We ran toward the chopper pad and slid down the embankment on the north side. I wasn't positive that Madigan had her, but I was reasonably certain she wouldn't try to escape back to the VC. It was very possible Madigan had observed me leave the hooch and decided to try some of his disjointed charm on her again.

Cino stepped cautiously to a plywood door hinged on a wall beneath the elevated chopper pad. He leaned and peeked through a crack at the edge of the door. I lowered my rifle to rest on the sling and eased beneath the lip of the pad, trying to see over his head.

Cassidy turned abruptly into me. "She's in there," he whispered through clinched teeth. "Take a look and you'll see how sick this pukin' anus is."

The first thing I saw was flickers of light shining on Lee-lin's tear-glossed face. She was strung up by her arms against a wall. Her legs were tied wide apart—spread-eagle. The T-shirt was completely cut up the center, fully exposing her otherwise naked body. Muck was caked on her legs and arms like she'd been dragged to his hooch through the mud.

Madigan stepped in front of her, holding a knife in one hand and a pistol in the other. "Now, you little commie cunt, it's just you and me!" he snarled, jabbing the knife point into her nipple.

"Aheeee!" she screamed, trying helplessly to jerk away from the biting point.

A napalm rage exploded through me. I lunged against the flimsy door, shattering it.

Madigan whirled toward me, dropping his knife. "You're fuckin' dead!" he shouted, jutting the pistol at me.

I dropped beneath the point-blank aim and rammed into his gut. Two earsplitting shots boomed over my head. I drove forward, pinning his struggling body to the wall. The heel of his pistol hammered my head.

"Freeze, anus! I'll rip you into a pile of shit!" Cino shouted.

The pounding on my head stopped. I quickly grabbed his pistol hand and twisted it viciously.

He screamed in pain and dropped the forty-five.

I jabbed my open hand around his neck and jammed

him against the wall. His sour, gasping breath spewed snot over his quivering lips as my fingers dug deeper into his throat. "Die! Die! You scum punk!"

"Yon-cee, no! No, Yon-cee!" Lee-lin's voice flooded my senses. I turned quickly toward her pleading face, releasing the limp body from my grasp.

Madigan wilted to the floor like a stunned cobra.

"Why . . . why did you stop me?" I muttered through labored breath.

"You no be an-e-mal, Yon-cee. I'm no wan you be same-same dis *lo-dit* an-e-mal!"

I stooped to pick up the knife and cut the ties on her feet. As I freed her arms she fell forward, lacing her arms around me. I hugged her shivering body against mine, combing my fingers through her wet hair.

"I'm think you number one, Yon-cee. You *beaucoup* number one," she said, gripping me tighter.

I kissed the top of her head. "I think you're number one too, Lee-lin. Number-focking-one!"

Pushing her gently away, I reached and pulled the cravat from my neck and wrapped it over her bleeding breast. I tied it in back, then glanced at Cino, who was kneeling over Madigan's wheezing body. "When he gets coherent, tie his hands.

"This may be the first time in military history an NCO has relieved an officer . . . but that's what I'm doing."

"Roger, Brett. I saw it. He flat-ass tried to kill you!" Cino reached to pick up my hat and examine it. "I'm not going to tell you how close he came, but this should give you some idea." He held my hat up with the end of his finger poking through a bullet hole.

I took the hat and looked down at Cino. "A good friend of mine named Swede Jensen once told me that close only counts in horseshoes, hand grenades, and nuclear bombs. This lieutenant is not only an undiscovered maniac, he's also a bad shot. That's totally unforgivable.''

I found a pair of Madigan's fatigues on a shelf and passed them to Lee-lin. ''Here, these will come closer to fitting you than mine will. And here's a towel to wipe yourself off with.''

As Lee-lin cleaned up and put on the clothing, Cassidy and I lifted the lieutenant onto a bunk and secured his hands and feet. After a moment he began to regain consciousness.

I stood looking down at him. ''Can you hear me, Lieutenant?'' His eyes cast a dizzy roll from side to side as he nodded. ''Hear this: You are being relieved of your command by me. I'm acting solely on my own discretion without influence from anyone. Do you understand that?''

He blinked and grunted.

''The reason you are being relieved is for attempted murder, attempted rape, and torturing a prisoner. Lance Corporal Cassidy will testify to the events that occurred here.'' I glanced at Cino. ''Is that right, Cino?''

''Right!''

I picked up Madigan's pistol from the floor, flipped the safety on, and tucked it into my belt. Cino found a poncho and fastened it over the gaping doorway.

''Cino, I'm taking Lee-lin over to the medic bunker to get her treated and let Zak know what's happened. How about you staying here with this *lo-dit*. I won't be long.''

''Okay, Brett. Got it handled. What's a *lo-dit*?''

''It's Vietnamese for 'asshole.' I thought everyone knew that.''

Chapter 20

When I arrived at the medical bunker with Lee-lin, Zakary was asleep. I asked the medic to treat the knife cut on Lee-lin's breast, then knelt next to the gunny.

"Zak, it's Yancy," I said, nudging him gently. "Zak, wake up."

He awoke abruptly. "Yancy, what's up? What's wrong?"

"Sorry to wake you, Zak. We've had some problems with Madigan. I had to relieve him and—"

He frowned. "You what? You . . . relieved . . . the lieutenant?" His gaze shifted to Lee-lin, seated near the medic with her shirt off. "Am I seein' things? Who's that?"

"Her name is—"

"Hold it! Hold everything! This is Firebase Zulu, and it's October, '69, right?"

"Right."

"And you've just relieved the lieutenant of his command. Did I hear that right?" he said, groping for a cigarette.

"Roger all the above, Zak."

"Now, who's that?" He nodded toward the girl.

"This is the prisoner I told you about earlier. Her name is Lee-lin Hoa. I've determined she isn't VC. She was taken by the Cong about a year ago—kidnaped."

In a few moments I'd given Zakary the details leading to my decision to remove Madigan from command. Lee-lin watched and listened to my explanation.

"Excusing me, Yon-cee," she interrupted. "I'm nee tell dis man sum-ting, please."

"Go ahead, Lee-lin."

Her eyebrows rose with emphasis as she spoke. "Sur, I Lee-lin Hoa. VC taking me from Quang Tri one year go. Dis man, Yon-cee, is saving me from VC and take care me.

"Dat *trung-'uy* is try focking me and him tie me and cut me. You see?" she said, holding her slit breast out to Zak in both hands. "You see? Dis supor *lo-dit* is *dinky-dow* and him try kill Yon-cee for stop him focking me. He number ten-thou and—"

"Okay, okay, Lee, I think he under—"

"I'm no fini please! I'm sum-ting more say."

"You go right ahead, little lady," Zak encouraged.

She bowed her head, then looked up and spoke slowly. "I'm hear VC talk say A-mer-ca sol-dur do many bad tings. Dat why dae wan kill A-mer-ca sol-dur. I'm no wan believe dem.

"But, now I'm—" She looked down at the knife cut on her nipple, then glanced back at us with sad eyes. "Now, I'm ting maybe VC can be right. VC never do dis to me. Yon-cee, him number-one man. Him telling me not all A-mer-ca like *trung-'uy*, I'm ting . . ." A tear rolled down her cheek.

She drew her lip slowly into her mouth and brushed the tear away. "I'm ting, I no wan my country, Vietnam, having man like *trung-'uy* come here. I wishing you pleasing sen him away, Vietnam.''

The gunny propped up on his elbow. "Yancy's right, Lee. Many good Americans have come here to try to give your country a better, a free, way of life. A lot of our men die here for your country.

"We have a sayin' in America: 'One bad apple don't spoil the whole barrel.' You see, the lieutenant is a bad apple. Try not to judge all Americans by his way. Could you do that for me?''

She glanced at me, then smiled at Zak. "Yes, sur. Yon-cee say him su-por as-ho, and you say him bad a-pel.''

Zak grinned and took a draw on his smoke. "I think Yancy's description is probably better, Lee." He looked over and grinned.

"Brett, this busted leg kinda puts me in the out-of-order category. I couldn't hit my ass with both hands full of Ping-Pong paddles, right now. You're the next senior rankin' man on this hill. It looks like you'll need to run the show till we can get a chopper in here. You got any problems with that?" he said, raising an eyebrow at me.

"No problem, Zak. You've got a good team here."

He looked at the medic. "Nelson, as soon as you get that little lady bandaged up there, I want you to go tell the men that Yancy here is in charge till further notice.''

"Roger, Gunny," he said, pulling a bandage from an aid pouch.

"Brett, you can leave little Lee here with us. Where's Madigan, now?''

"In his hooch. Cassidy's guarding him.''

"Bring him over here, we'll guard him. That'll free

Cassidy up to help you. You're gonna need ever rifle on line you can muster.''

The muffled pop of an illumination round brought Zak's eyes upward, then back to me. ''And tell the mortar crew to go easy on those lume rounds. We're runnin' low and we won't get a resupply till this weather breaks. I'll get a message off to headquarters and let them know what our situation is.''

When I returned to Madigan's hooch I found Cino sitting cross-legged by the lieutenant's bunk, blowing marijuana smoke into his face. Madigan's eyes rolled lazily over at me like a slow-motion satellite gliding toward the dark side of the moon.

Cino looked around at me with a grin. ''I've been tellin' Lieutenant *Lo-dit* here about the importance of staying in touch with himself. He's not sayin' much. I think he's depressed or something.''

Cino took a draw on the joint. ''Are you depressed, Lieutenant? You've been a bad boy,'' he said, blowing a puff into Madigan's face.

''Snuff that joint and untie his legs. I'm taking him over to Zak. He'll guard him.''

He stood and held the reefer out to me. ''You want some of this?''

''No. And, I don't want to see you or anybody else using that shit tonight.''

''Hey, there's nothing wrong with a little grass.''

''Get this, Cino. I don't mind you getting stoned when you're off the clock. But there's a time and place for it, and this isn't it. That stuff slows you down—impairs judgment.'' I winked. ''I need you and everybody else playing with a full deck tonight, partner.''

Cassidy dropped the joint to the floor and stepped on it.

After untying Madigan's feet we pulled him upright from the bunk. He wobbled, trying to stand. Placing a firm grip under his arm, I led him to the door.

"Where . . . where we goin'?" the lieutenant mumbled.

I looked at Cino. "I'll take him over to the medic bunker and leave him with Zak. You go check the guard positions and find out if anyone's seen any movement. Meet me back at Mole's position.

"Oh, and tell the mortar pit to slack off on lume rounds. Tell them to pour it on if we get hit; otherwise pop a round about every fifteen or twenty minutes. Roger?"

"Roger, Brett."

When I entered the bunker with the lieutenant, Nelson was gone. I checked the binding on Madigan's wrist to insure it was tight, then carefully eased him into a sitting position in the corner—in clear view of Lee and Zak.

"Here's his forty-five, Zak," I said, pulling the pistol from my belt and handing it to the gunny. "I don't think he'll be any problem. He's still in a daze."

Zak placed the pistol aside, then looked directly at Madigan and spoke with a matter-of-fact tone. "Lieutenant, we've seen fit to relieve you of command. You are now in custody and will remain that way. Do you understand?"

Madigan lowered his head without replying. Lee-lin stood and moved close to me.

I rested my hand on her shoulder. "Lee-lin, I need to know where the VC assembled—massed—before the attack. Can you tell me where?"

She thought for a moment. "Other side big hill from where I come."

I looked at Zak. "She's talking about Hill Ten-fifteen.

I'm going to call in an arty strike on the east side of that hill.''

"Good idea. Have 'em walk it down, north to south, at twenty-meter intervals along the base of the hill. I figure they're grouped along the hill base. Henderson has the grids you'll need to call the fire mission. He's in the commo bunker.''

"Yon-cee, I'm liking go wid you. Maybe helping you. Is okay?''

I caressed the nape of her neck. "Thank you, but you will help me best by staying here with Zak and watching this *lo-dit*. Okay?''

I walked to the door, then turned and looked at her concerned face. "And if we get hit, don't come outside, no matter what. One of our men may mistake you for VC and shoot you. I want you to be back home in one piece in a day or two. Understand?''

She smiled. "Rog-ee. I'm under-stan.''

Moments later I'd called an artillery fire mission. I hurried to Mole's position to await the barrage.

The stink of scorched rat tail bit my nostrils when I entered the bunker. The incessant rain had begun to seep into the fortification, turning the floor into ankle-deep mud. Cino was waiting with Mole.

Both Marines had their weapons jutted out the firing port as they peered into the rainy darkness.

"I've got an arty strike coming," I said, moving to Cino's side. "How many M-60 gunners do we have around here?''

"Three," he answered.

I was surprised there wasn't one in, or at least near, this bunker. "Cino, what do you think about relocating one of those machine guns in here?''

"Sounds good," Cassidy replied, turning toward the

door. "I'll go get Sure-shot Shilo. He's the best. Be right back."

Mole turned to me, whispering, "Cino told me about what Madigan did to Lee-lin. I—I think that's terrible. I'm glad you relieved him. Can you actually do that? I didn't know a sergeant could do that."

I whispered back, "Well, it's not in the books, Mole. But, it was the right thing to do. Why are we whispering?"

"I—I don't know," he said, tilting his head upward.

"Me neither."

"You know, she reminds me of my departed sister. Lee-lin, I mean. She's a nice girl. Right?"

"You're right. She's great, Mole. And it makes me feel kind of good that we're out here on freedom's anvil. We're helping to beat the Communist bastards off this corner of the globe for kids like her."

He turned to me and whispered again. "Brett, will you join me in a word of prayer?"

I glanced at his imploring, dark eyes. "Sure, Mole. Fire away, buddy."

Mackenzie steadied his rifle on the sandbag support, then folded his hands over the rear sights and bowed his head.

I kept my gaze focused out into the black rain. Inwardly I was wondering what was taking the fire mission I'd called for so long.

Thunder cracked as Mole's words drifted over me. "Our Father who art in heaven, hallowed be thy name. I'll shorten this tonight, Lord, because I'm on line right now as you probably already know.

"Thank you for bringing little Lee-lin into our fold and saving her from the Communist bas—I mean, heathens. Please bless every Marine on this hill in our time of need, and, particularly, Brett Yancy, who is not a Marine . . .''

I looked over at Mole's bowed head wondering why he needed to single me out by name.

''. . . And forgive Lieutenant Madigan, for he knows not what he does. And bless my parents and be with my sister, Janice, who is still in the hospital with muscular dystrophy. You have taken Judy into your heavenly embrace, and I—I understand it is part of your—your master plan, Lord. But—but please God, let Janice live and carry—carry on your divine work here on earth. I love her so very much.

''I—I ask these things in Christ's name. Amen.''

He raised his tear-glossed face and smiled at me.

I put my arm around him and gently squeezed his shoulder. ''You're a heck of a guy, Mackenzie. I'm proud to be out here with you, partner.''

Chapter 21

At 0120 hours the wild shriek of a 155-mm artillery round cut through the night. It impacted with the roar of earth-bound thunder on the far side of Hill 1015.

"That's a great sound, ain't it?" Cassidy said, hurrying into the bunker. Grinning, he crowded between Mole and me like a youngster at a Fourth-of-July celebration. "I used to love that sound when I worked FO. Not the explosion so much, but that special kind of racket the round makes tearing through the night.

"A gunny on Hill Eight-eight-one described it perfect. He said it sounded like a scared squirrel running through dry leaves."

I hadn't seen Cassidy this excited since we discovered that Jacob Ray was alive.

Another projectile streaked through the darkness. I listened closer.

"He's right. It does sound like a squirrel running through leaves." I glanced at Cino as the round boomed in the distance.

"Dry leaves!" Cino corrected. "There's a difference, Brett."

"Okay, dry leaves. Where's the M-60 gunner, Shilo?"

"Be here in a minute," Cassidy answered.

"Y'all give me a hand over here," I said, walking toward the bunker entrance.

We removed a dozen sandbags from a section of the revetment wall to form a window with a good field of fire for the M-60. When we finished that, Cassidy busied himself routing the claymore wires and generators to a central location near Mole's position.

A moment later, the tall figure of a man lugging an M-60 machine gun sloshed down the trench toward us. Linked belts of 7.62 ammo crisscrossed his poncho. He stooped, entering the bunker, then looked at the new firing port.

"I see you already got an office set up for me. Where's the coffeepot?" he said, glancing around with a quick smirk.

"You must be 'Sure-shot' Shilo. I'm Brett." I held my hand out, taking an ammo can from him and setting it below the window.

"Glad to meet you. I presume you want me and my instrument to entertain right here?" He slid the machine gun across the sandbags.

"Roger," I replied, noticing Cino carefully pull a Kaybar from beneath his poncho. He held the pointed end cupped in his grip while peering intensely toward the far end of the bunker.

Then he raised the knife slowly, and in one swift flick-of-wrist movement hurled the blade past Mole. A piercing screech rent the air as the knife plunged into its target.

"Chow time!" Cassidy blurted.

Squinting toward the dark upper corner of the bunker, I saw a huge, football-sized rat squirming—pinned to the wall. Cassidy's accuracy with a knife didn't amaze me as much as his ability to see the rodent in the first place.

Mole grinned as Cino hurried to his victim. "Good shot, Cino."

Without comment, Cassidy quickly pulled the bloody rat down. He cut the long black tail off and stuck it in his pocket.

By 0200 hours the artillery fire ceased. We hadn't heard a peep from Charlie. Cassidy had cooked his prey and squatted in the corner gnawing on fresh rat ribs. His teeth tore into the ribs like a pit bull attacking a mailman's leg.

"I don't know how you can eat that," Mole said, looking down at Cino.

Cino spoke between swallows. "Good stuff. You don't know what you're missing. Besides, it's all in your mind. Remember when you were a kid, and your mom tried to get you to eat broccoli, and you hated the idea? But after you tried it, it wasn't so bad. Same with rat."

"Yeah, I remember broccoli," Shilo said. "And I still don't like that shit!"

Cino dragged the back of his hand across his lips. "Rats are survivors, strong. That's why they're so nutritious. Did you know they can actually digest Brillo pads?"

"That's fantastic," Shilo said, turning away. "I like Brillo pads even less than broccoli."

Mole looked around at me. "Brett, I—I am kind of hungry. Do you have any more of those—those spaghetti and meat sauce rations?"

"Sure do, partner. I'm going out and check the other positions. I'll bring you one on my way back here."

Moving across the crest of the hill, I saw the small tattered American flag fluttering above the commo shed.

I skirted the perimeter and checked several sentry positions. Nobody had seen anything.

My last stop was the howitzer emplacement located on the western slope. The fire team, two men, informed me that the shell extractor of the 105-mm gun was inoperative. They had to manually remove each expended shell from the breech by using an old jeep tire tool.

The manual method of shell extraction significantly slowed them down. They had one beehive round loaded and ready to go, in case an assault came from their side of the hill.

The beehive round was the best short-range antipersonnel ordnance they could select for their limited situation. The gun was aimed straight down the mouth of the most likely zone of enemy approach.

I'd seen beehive rounds fired before. The round hurled eight thousand small winged darts, called flechettes, over a hundred-meter area. The flying steel ripped through anything in its path.

I helped the gun team place two claymores on the front side of the gun as a secondary surprise for any VC that made it through the beehive nightmare. But since Charlie didn't know that the howitzer was malfunctioning, it was my guess that he'd consider the western slope as the least likely avenue of approach. The howitzer had been strategically positioned on the more vulnerable west slope as a deliberate deterrent for enemy assault.

The southern side of Zulu was too steep to accommodate an en masse attack. The northern portion had "frigid-bitch," waist-high wire layers so deep a ground hog couldn't weave his way through it without being ripped to shreds.

I was certain that if another attack came tonight it

would be straight up the eastern slope where they'd come from earlier.

I thought back to the recent artillery strike. The absence of secondary explosions during the fire mission told me it was possible Charlie had reassembled in another area after the initial assault. But I wasn't going to risk putting a patrol down there in this weather to find out.

On my way back I stopped in Ray's Alpine Chalet to pick up a ration for Mole. While in the hooch I packed the radio and the sawed-off M-79 in my ruck and took it with me. I planned to use the radio to initiate a three-way communications net with the commo bunker, the howitzer team, and myself.

When I exited the hooch I noticed that the rain had diminished to a light drizzle, but now the ground fog was beginning to thicken. By the time I got back to the east bunker the fog was so dense I could barely see the trench outline.

As I entered the bunker I saw Cassidy and Shilo at the M-60 window. Mole was at the other firing port with his head leaned forward on the sandbags. I didn't know if he was praying again or sleeping.

I set my ruck aside, pulled out the ration, and nudged him. "Here's that LRP you wanted."

He raised his head abruptly. "Oh . . . oh, thank you."

Cassidy moved near me. "We're sittin' smack dab in the middle of a big cloud right now. We can't see nothing. You want me to go out and make a little sneak and peek recon?"

The casual tone of his suggestion made it sound like he was going for a stroll in the park, not a perilous solo recon knee-deep in VC. I studied his face.

The idea was good. Right now we needed any intel we

could get—there wasn't a better, more experienced man for the task.

As a lume round popped I looked out into the dark gray curtain of fog. The flare revealed nothing more than a dim glow in the fog.

"All right, Cino, one condition."

"What's that?"

I pointed to the PRC-25 stuffed in my ruck. "You take that radio and make a commo check with Henderson every twenty minutes."

"Hold it, Brett! You know how I feel about gear. Hangs—"

"Hangs up in the bush. I know, but I don't give a damn. You do it my way, or not at all."

Mole interjected. "Why not do it Brett's way? That way you can let us know if you spot something or need help."

I glanced at Mole, half astonished by his perception, then looked back at Cassidy.

He scowled, looking at the radio like it was a pill he had to swallow. He muttered while taking his poncho off. "Okay, okay, I'll take the damn—darn thing!"

Shilo spoke in a wry voice. "Just think of it as broccoli, Cino."

Chapter 22

I sat in the smoky communications hut with Kirk Henderson waiting for Cino to make his first commo check. It was now 0245 hours—he'd been gone for thirty-eight minutes without calling in.

"Relax, Sarge. He's probably just lost track of time," Kirk said, glancing at me.

"That's it, dammit! He doesn't have a watch. That's why," I said, remembering the rescue mission we'd been on. Cino knew the moment I told him to make a radio check every twenty minutes that he had a built-in excuse to avoid it because he didn't have a watch. I'd forgotten all about it.

Henderson shrugged. "Well, that explains it. We'll probably be hearing from him anytime now."

A low, booming noise rumbled outside—I recognized the sound.

"What's that?" he said, looking upward, then back at me.

"Grenade. I asked the guard on the south wall to toss one down into the dump every now and then to keep sappers from trying to slip up that side."

I looked at my watch again. "I'm going to go over

and check on Zak. If Cassidy calls in while I'm gone, tell him—"

"Wait a minute; I hear something," Kirk said, keying the mike. "This is Zulu, go ahead, Nighthawk . . . Roger, he's right here. Stand by."

I took the handset from Henderson. "This is Zulu, over."

Cino's voice was barely a whisper. "That arty didn't do the trick. We gotta bunch of November-Victor-Alphas down here. They're comin' up the trail on the northeast side of the saddle. I see rocket tubes. You copy?"

"Roger, Nighthawk, copy. Good job. Get on back in here pronto, Tonto."

Silence. I keyed again. "Nighthawk, this is Zulu. I said get your ass back in here now! You copy that?"

"Keep your shirt on. I'm comin' your way."

I passed the handset to Kirk. "Call base and let them know we've been hit and we're expecting a major assault any—"

Suddenly two earth-jarring explosions shook the bunker.

"That's mortar!" Kirk yelled, fumbling to change the frequency on his radio.

"Get that message through!" I grabbed my CAR-15 and bolted into the fog-veiled night.

Automatic weapons fire rattled from the west side. Cino's intel indicated the attack would be coming from the east.

I sprinted to the howitzer emplacement and saw the dim profiles of several Marines returning fire along the wall. A teeming volume of mortar lashed earsplitting explosions through the fog, heaving mud and debris everywhere.

I dove into a crevice near the huddled gun crew. The

acrid stench of exploded powder stained the air as the wet earth trembled beneath me.

"Hold that beehive till I give you a go!" I yelled.

Easing my head around a corner I peered into the field of fire. Trip flares spewed light along the fog base, revealing a dozen black-clad figures crawling toward us.

I jabbed my muzzle downrange, triggering an oscillating burst of fire. The Marines along the wall riveted a blazing chorus of automatic fire into the dark figures.

I hunkered, yanked a grenade from my shoulder strap, and tossed a high hook shot over the wall. Another mortar round exploded—east side.

"You wanna hit 'em with this beehive?" a gunner yelled.

A red flag flipped into my mind. Cino had told me he saw NVA moving up into the saddle. The targets we'd just laid out were VC—half of them weren't even returning fire.

"Negative, don't fire," I yelled back to the gunner. "This is a fucking diversion!"

The incoming stopped. I shouted to the men on the wall. "Four of you come with me!"

I gripped the gunner's shoulder. "Watch this zone close. If they bring it on strong go ahead and hit 'em with your best shit! I'm moving to the east side."

I turned and motioned for the Marines to follow me. We moved across the hill slowly, headed for the east bunker.

Successive lume rounds popped overhead, casting undulating light through the engulfing cloud cover. I looked toward my hooch. Ray's Alpine Chalet and Card Parlor was a lumped shambles. It had taken a direct hit.

"So much for magic chicken feet," I muttered to myself.

A Marine shouted, pointing south, "Look at that. Them motherfuckers got Hanna with those last rounds! Now where we gonna shit?"

"You're probably gonna shit in your pants before this night is over!" another man answered.

We weaved through puddles, craters, and debris looking for signs of enemy. As we traversed the hill the wafting stink of combat alerted my senses. Both the commo and medical bunkers appeared to have survived the mortar pounding we'd just taken.

As we neared the mortar pit I wanted to tell the crew to start pouring HE, high-explosive rounds, down into the saddle. But it was possible Cino was down there. I couldn't risk it.

When we reached the east side I signaled for the Marines with me to take up trench positions, then I hurried into the bunker.

Shilo's quick words greeted me. "What the fuck's been happening on the west side?"

"A diversion, but they must've had their signals mixed up or they'd be on us by now. Is Cassidy back yet?"

Mole answered, "No, no, we haven't seen him. Did— did he check in with you? I'm worried about him."

"Roger, Mole. He's on his way in; says we got *beaucoup* NVA massing in the saddle," I said, tapping Shilo's shoulder. I pointed to his left out the window.

"It's my guess they'll be coming from the direction. Watch for Cassidy before you put anything downrange."

I turned to Mole. "I'm headed over to give Zak a sit-rep. If Cino gets back while I'm gone, tell him to get over to the mortar pit and have them start dropping HE. He knows where."

While making my way to the medic bunker two more enemy rounds thundered on the north side. The low level of noise indicated they'd fallen outside the "frigid-bitch" wire barrier.

I shouted my name entering the bunker. "It's Yancy!"

Lee-lin lit up like a Christmas tree. "Yon-cee, you okay?"

"I'm okay, but we need to look for a new apartment, darlin'."

Zak frowned. "Sounded like all hell breakin' loose out there!"

"Roger," I said, glancing at the empty corner. "Where's Madigan?"

"Awe, he started bitchin' and moanin' 'bout needin' to take a shit, right before that incoming hit us. I had Nelson escort 'em over to Hanna. They oughta be back in—"

"Zak, Hanna took a direct hit!"

"Holy shit! You mean . . . shit, how 'bout Nelson?"

Chapter 23

Minutes later we found Nelson's body. He'd been blown halfway across the compound. In addition to being perforated with shrapnel, his neck was broken. We placed him in a body bag and carried him to Madigan's hooch for storage.

After returning to the ruins of Hanna, several Marines helped me dig through the mingled mass of splintered boards and shit, searching for the lieutenant. While tossing a piece of wood aside, a man said, "I don't think we're gonna find nothing but bits and pieces of Madman in here, that is, if we find any fuckin' thing at all."

As I stepped into the wreckage pulling boards away, a Marine grabbed my shoulder. "Careful, Sarge, there's a twenty-foot hole under those boards. I know, I helped dig it!"

When we cleared the area that covered the sump hole, I knelt and directed the beam of my flashlight down the shaft. The fetor watered my eyes. I coughed and blinked while moving the light beam back and forth over the debris lodged in the bottom of the cesspool.

Finally, I caught a glimpse of a boot sticking out of the muck. Leaning to hold the light farther down the shaft I saw a portion of leg attached to the boot. I didn't know if Madigan was in one piece, but part of him was here.

Cassidy blurted at me, "What are you looking for, Yancy? Lose a contact?"

I glanced across the rubble at his smirking face. "Glad to see you finally made it back! No, I lost a lieutenant. But I just found him."

I stood and turned to the man nearest me. "How about getting some rope and making a slip loop in one end. Lower it down and try to loop it over his foot. I'll send another man over to help y'all pull him out."

Cassidy stepped forward through the fog to look into the hole.

A Marine said, "Hey, Sarge, for now, why not just leave 'im in the—"

I turned to face him. "You wouldn't want to be left buried upside-down in six feet of shit, would you? Cino, let's get over to the mortar pit!" I said, walking away.

Cassidy hurried behind me. "Hey, you were a little tough on Butch, weren't you?"

I plodded ahead. "Just tellin' it like it is. That's all. What took you so damn long getting back here?"

"Well, you see, I met this NVA who was laggin' behind the others. So I asked 'im if he'd like to trade some baseball cards with me."

I halted and narrowed my eyes looking into his.

Cassidy flashed a vicious, wide-eyed grin at me. He jerked his Kaybar out and held the point beneath his chin. "The little prick said he didn't like baseball . . . so I killed 'im!"

The look on Cino's face was somewhere between horrific and hilarious. "Cassidy, you've been out in the fog too long. Have you been smoking those left-wing Luckies again?''

Glancing down, he slid his knife into the scabbard. ''Nope. A buddy of mine told me there's a time and place for that shit, I mean, stuff—and this ain't it!''

''What's the situation out there?'' I nodded east.

''It's like nothin' I've seen before. I'll tell you this, Brett. Chuck is puttin' together one big show for us.''

I turned. ''Come on, Tonto. Tell it to me on the way. Let's get this mortar pit dealing a little retribution on those antibaseball pricks.''

Cassidy's assessment of the enemy situation was precise, and without exaggeration. Although he hadn't been able to penetrate very far into the lower area, he did see enough to clearly indicate that the enemy was marshaling for a major assault on us.

He estimated that they had a dozen rocket teams and approximately four hundred personnel—VC and NVA. We'd already learned from the previous attack that they also had a mortar squad out there somewhere.

After assessing our ammo stockpile I found that we had 153 rounds of 82-mm HE mortar, 22 lume rounds, 6 cases of M-79, HE, and Willie-Pete, and a dozen cases of M-26 grenades. In addition, we had a case of claymore mines, and plenty of 5.56 and 7.62 ammo.

The howitzer team had no shortage on ammo, but with their limited firepower output I couldn't count it as functionally beneficial to our situation.

We now had two KIA, one wounded, seventeen warm-bodied Marines, myself, and a little girl. Without Nelson, we didn't even have a medic.

After a brief skull session with Zak about our situation, we both agreed that it was an Alamo stand. The cloud cover prevented tac-air, and right now the enemy was so close we couldn't call in arty without jeopardizing ourselves.

I stood and took a last gulp of coffee. I'd given Zak the no sugar-coating details of our firepower inventory as well as Cino's estimate of the enemy strength. His face reflected concern—Lee-lin's expression mirrored Zak's.

Throughout our discussion a question had been kicking around inside me. I didn't like sounding negative but I needed an answer.

I knelt next to Lee-lin as I spoke. "Zak, just as a matter of contingency, do you have an escape and evasion plan for Zulu?"

He grimaced, trying to turn onto his side. "Negative! I suggested planning one, but the lieutenant wouldn't have anything to do with it."

Having witnessed Madigan in action, I wasn't surprised that he didn't want anything to do with retreat. But Special Forces A-team and recon procedure considered E and E vital. All A-teams throughout Vietnam had both a primary and an alternate E and E plan.

I pulled the map from my pocket and pointed to Zulu. "It's not likely, but if we have to beat feet, I figure our best bet is straight down the south slope into the dump. The steep slope here will facilitate an easy slide through the mud.

"After assembly, we move southeast and intersect the route Cassidy and I took to Enola Hetero. Then we'd head straight into Khe Sanh. There's an old bunker there where we found Ray."

I looked up at Zak's frowning face. "What do you think?"

He rubbed his whiskers. "Well, truth is, there ain't

no good ways outa here. But, if we use that south side, we'd better prep it good with HE, first.''

"Can't do it!" As soon as I'd blurted the words out I realized I was starting to sound like Cino.

"What I'm saying is, Zak, any HE prep on that side of the hill is waving a flag over our intended direction of escape. I already have a sentry over there dropping a frag off that side to deter a sapper probe, so maybe it'll help keep the area clear. I gotta get back on line. Give it some thought.''

"Roger, Yancy. Say, you got any more of that morphine handy?''

I stood, looked down at his grimacing face, and lied. "No, I don't. Sorry, Zak. Try and get some rest. I'll be back later.''

I still had one Syrette of morphine left in my aid pouch, but if we ended up having to take him down the hill and bounce him through the jungle—I knew he'd need it a lot more then.

All things considered, I didn't feel like we were going to have to run. Cassidy's intel had eliminated Chuck's surprise element. In addition, we had the terrain advantage and a good defensive position, not to mention a hill full of seasoned, kick-ass Leathernecks ready to fight. If Charlie wanted this hill, he was going to pay dearly for it.

Before exiting the bunker I looked around at the gunny. "By the way, Zak, since Madigan's taken that hit, well . . . I figure there's no purpose in throwing the book at his coffin. If you know what I mean?

"All his family is going to have is a flag and a tombstone to cling to. Might as well let them believe he died a hero.''

Zak tried to smile. "Yeah, I was kinda thinkin' the same way." His eyes traveled to Lee-lin.

She darted a glance to both of us as she spoke. "I'm think I under-stan what you say. Him mamasan only be hurting if she knowing him bad a-pel."

I winked. "You know, Lee-lin, you're very astute. Which is another way of saying, I think you're number-focking-one!"

Smiling, she stood and pointed at Zak. "I also pretty good nurse. Don you worry, Yon-cee, I'm take care dis man, Pak."

I gave a quick, smiling salute and headed out of the bunker.

Chapter 24

On my way back to the east side I picked up three clay-mores at the ammo dump and put them in an empty sandbag.

As I sloshed into the east-side bunker I became aware that the mortar pit had ceased fire.

"What are you going to do with those?" Mole asked, watching me remove the mines from the sandbag.

"This is an insurance policy," I said, looking around for Cassidy. Then, something caught my attention. Shilo was standing at his firing window adjusting a small reel-type tape recorder.

Curious, I stepped closer looking at the speakers. "What's this, music to fight by?" I halfway expected him to say it was the Marine Corps hymn.

He positioned a small speaker on each side of his machine gun, then answered, "It's the 'Gary Owen.' George Custer's fightin' theme."

"You should have joined the Air Cavalry. That's their music."

"Yeah, maybe, but Custer was born in my hometown, Monroe, Michigan. That makes it my music too. Did you ever see that movie *They Died With Their Boots On*, with Errol Flynn?''

"Sure did," I said, remembering. "I'd guess, between TV and the theater, I saw that movie five or six times."

"Yeah, me too. There was just something about it. Maybe it was the bagpipes and bugles, or maybe it just captured my imagination for fighting. Of course, it could have been because I grew up in Custer country. Who knows?''

I looked at Mole. "Where's Cino?"

"Oh, oh, I forgot to tell you. Henderson came—came over here looking for you. He—he said he wasn't able to make commo with base because that incoming tore his antenna off the roof, and . . ." Mole's sleepy eyes looked up at me. "What was the question you asked? I forgot."

"I asked, where's Cino?"

"Oh, yeah, that's where he is."

"Where?"

Shilo looked over his shoulder. "Cino's helping Kirk get his antenna back up. I ain't heard a mortar round for a couple of minutes. They're probably lettin' their tube cool down."

Looking around for the PRC-25, I noticed it was gone. It appeared that Cassidy had adopted it. I'd have to wait until he got back before I could set up the three-way commo net.

Mole turned around to peer out his window again. I could see he was having trouble staying awake. "Why don't you relax awhile, Mole? Get a little shut-eye. Shilo and I can keep watch," I said, taking a small roll of time fuse from my ruck.

"Okay, thanks, Brett. It's—it's been a long night. I'll just go over to the hooch and get a blanket."

"Uh, wait a minute, Mole." I told him about the NVA urban annihilation alterations on our chalet. He fell back against the wall like I'd slapped him.

A tear rolled off his cheek. "Oh, no!" he said, sliding down to a sandbag seat. "All—all my letters from home were in—in there." He looked up with a lost expression.

"Try not to worry, Mole. Come daylight, we'll dig through the rubble and find them. There wasn't a fire. They're still in there somewhere, partner. Get some rest."

He drew his knees up and folded his arms across them. He lowered his head onto his arms, then looked up abruptly. "How's—how's Lee-Lin? Is—is she okay?"

"She's fine," I said, placing the claymores into my ruck. Then I began cutting the time fuse into three two-foot lengths. I attached a plastic fuse igniter to each piece and attached a blasting cap to each of the other ends, taping them tightly.

"What are you putting together there?" Shilo asked.

"Time pencils. It's an expedient device to detonate a claymore without using the generator and wire." Shilo rubbed his chin and watched as I carefully wrapped each pencil into a cravat and placed them in my ruck.

"You mind if I ask a dumb question, Yancy?"

I set the ruck aside. "The only dumb question is an unasked question."

"Well, why would anybody need one of those time pencil things to blow a claymore when you already got a hand generator?"

I placed the small M-79 along with several rounds onto a shelf below the firing-port window. "Elementary. If—"

Suddenly a chorus of howls, screams, and yelps rent the fog-cloaked night. Mackenzie scrambled to the window. Shilo latched a grip on his M-60 as the invisible, droning wave of racket rolled closer.

"Those bastards sound like the Demon Tabernacle Choir!" Shilo yelled.

I flipped my selector switch to full auto and jabbed the muzzle over the sandbags. The split-second swish of a rocket streaked over the bunker. Then another.

Lume popped overhead, followed by the thunder of our mortar explosions in the distance. The enemy rocket rounds were aimed too high—they'd gone over us.

"Give these *lo-dit*s some good fuckin' music," I yelled at Shilo.

As the first spirited bars of the "Gary Owen" pitched a high bagpipe-and-bugle rhythm into the night, a bright current of enemy muzzle flashes stretched across the brume. The blaring sound of Shilo's tape drowned out the ominous enemy chants.

His M-60 erupted in violent symphony with a dozen M16s riveting high-volume fire into the smoky onslaught.

My adrenaline pumped as I triggered a long burst into the dark hoards of NVA emerging from the mask of fog. Khaki-clad bodies jerked and twisted from the biting pelts of American lead hurling through the wire. They wilted in clumps, some throwing themselves into our concertina as dying human bridges for the mass of second-wave attackers.

Mackenzie fumbled to grab a claymore generator. "Should I—I blow the—"

"Do it!"

The claymore blast boomed like the hot breath of Vulcan spitting a wicked glob of death into the enemy's face. The curtain of shrieking steel balls rolled a dozen NVA backward like chess pieces in a hurricane.

A screaming cloud of enemy swept in and over the heaps of dead—pressing onward into our fury of fire. Massive volumes of enemy lead drummed against the bunker wall like pellets of hail.

I ejected my magazine, jammed in another, and hit the bolt release just as I saw a body lurch upward from the wire field. He was clutching a grenade. When his arm drew back to throw, I spit a lethal burst of 5.56 into his head, ripping the top of his skull off like a tear-away towel.

Lead spewed into Shilo's firing port, shattering his speakers to bits. He fell away clutching his arm. "I'm hit!" he groaned.

I yanked a cravat from my neck and jumped back, grabbing his arm. Blood coursed from his bicep. I quickly wrapped the cloth around it, tightened it, and pulled him forward. "All right, partner! Hit 'em again!"

He lunged to his machine gun, molding his finger into the trigger well. His hunched body moved in harmony with the M-60's jolting rhythm pouring a stream of tracers into the assault.

"They're over—over the wire!" Mole shouted.

I grabbed the preloaded M-79 and fired a white phosphorous round into the concertina. The round burst, spewing a cloud of white-hot flakes over the enemy. Agonized screams and yelps echoed through the night.

I broke the chamber open, flipped the expended shell out, and jammed an HE in. I snapped it shut, immediately firing at a line of figures hurtling over the littered clumps of dead NVA.

Suddenly a thunderous explosion jarred the bunker, throwing me to the floor. I quickly stumbled to my feet, peering through the stinking haze. The entire far end of the fortification had been ripped away by the rocket. I helped Shilo to his feet.

"Mole! Where's—"

"Help me! I'm—I'm—"

Shilo and I stumbled toward Mole's voice, clawing wet clumps of dirt and shredded sandbags away.

I heard mortar and rocket explosions raining in the distance. The rolling noise seemed to be coming from the west side. The stench of cordite raped the night air.

We grabbed Mole's arms and pulled him from beneath the caved-in dirt mass. "Mole, you okay?"

"I—I think, so. Where's—where's my gun? My gun?"

"Look out, Brett!" Shilo yelled.

I glanced upward to see an NVA, bayonet fixed, leaping from the gaping hole in the roof toward me.

I hurled a solid right fist into his face as he lunged the long-bladed steel at me. The blade jabbed through the side of my poncho and into the wall.

"You fuckin' missed, *lo-dit*!" I yelled, grabbing his head in both hands and twisting savagely. The horrid moan of death belched from his gasping mouth as his neck cracked in my frenzied grasp.

Shoving his limp carcass away, I screamed, "That's for Flight Time, you scum-suckin' glob of spit!"

Mole pawed at the dirt. "My gun . . . my gun!"

I quickly yanked the AK-47 loose from the wall, then pulled a banana magazine from the dead NVA's vest. "Forget it, Mackenzie, use my rifle. I'll use the AK!"

I handed my CAR-15 to Mole, then turned to Shilo, who was holding his M-60 at hip level, guarding the entrance.

I cast my poncho off and grabbed a grenade off my

web harness. I snatched the pin free and hurled the M-26 through the firing port.

Looking at Shilo's tight-jawed face, I said, "When that grenade goes off, let's get outside. It's street-fighting time. You hold this position, Mole, and blow that other claymore!"

When the grenade boomed, Shilo rushed forward out of the bunker and began blazing 7.62 toward the concertina.

I hurriedly reloaded the M-79, shoved it into my belt, and ran to join Shilo. A lume round radiated dim light above us, revealing blood streaming down his arm. He kept rattling oscillating fire along the east slope. Throngs of NVA melted into the wire.

I fired a hip-level AK burst into a crouched rocket launcher beyond the wire. Mole's claymore blast leveled all the NVA converging from the southeast corner. The wire was empty of standing targets.

Turning, I squinted through the swirling haze of smoke along the near trench line. Shilo's fire halted. A bloody pile of motionless NVA were strewn along the forward edge of the trench.

Two Marines lay twisted and dead, wilted forward over the trench lip. One man clutched his M16 trigger in his frozen grasp. Another Marine looked up at me with a bewildered gaze, then slowly leaned over the body of his dead comrade and wept.

Heavy automatic weapons fire suddenly erupted from the west side. I shouted to Shilo, who was loading another belt of ammo. "Y'all stay here! Hold this ground."

I turned and sprinted toward the intense firefight on the west side. Suddenly a pealing explosion cracked through the night, heaving the howitzer up and backward like a giant broomstick. Marines scurried away from the crumbling wall position. I caught a glimpse of Cassidy rallying a half-dozen Marines into a section of trench line. He still had the radio pack on his back.

A new ominous chorus of the "Demon Tabernacle Choir" roared from the lower western slope. I leapt into the trench next to Cassidy and peered in awe at the massive wave of VC and NVA emerging from the fog. I pulled the M-79 out and fired into the haze.

Cino darted a glanced at me. "Commo bunker took a hit. Kirk's dead! Mortar pit's out too!"

"Shit! How many we got on this side?" I shouted back.

"You're lookin' at it!"

"There's no fuckin' way we'll hold against this," I yelled while firing full-auto AK. "Cino, take one man, get to Zak, and move him and Lee-lin to the south wall. We're unassing this fuckin' hill!"

"Where's Mole?" he shouted, leaping from the trench.

"East bunker. I'll get him. Go!"

Cassidy tapped a man and motioned him out of the trench. They hurried away into the night. I flipped two successive grenades toward the wire, then shouted down the trench line above the racketing volume of weapons fire. "Hold these bastards a few minutes, then fall out to the south wall!"

"Roger, Sarge. We got it handled!"

As I leapt from the trench a round grazed my right earlobe. I felt the warm flow of blood on my neck as I sprinted east. In the haze I saw three silhouettes approaching my front. A step closer revealed Shilo and Mole running toward me, followed by another Marine.

"Sounded like you need us over there!" Shilo yelled.

"I've—I've got your ruck, Brett," Mole said through labored breaths.

"Y'all get to the south wall. Tear out a section of the sandbag wall. We're gonna E and E down that side!"

Mole looked stunned. "What's E and—"

"Move out, now!" I said, turning to sprint toward the medic bunker. I heard the growl of enemy cries above the roar of intense fire.

When I reached the medic bunker, Cassidy had rolled Zak over onto a spread poncho. He and the other Marine lifted him in the cradle of the poncho and moved him to the door.

Lee-lin was standing, holding Madigan's forty-five.

"You know how to use that, darlin'?" I said, glancing at the pistol.

"I'm think yes. Pak show me how."

"Okay, come on. Zak, we're going for a mud-slide ride."

We hurriedly carried Zak to the south wall. Shilo, Mole, and one other man were waiting for us when we arrived at the wall. I sent Shilo down first to take up a defensive position at the bottom.

As Shilo slid feet-first into the darkness he used the butt of the M-60 like a rudder stabbed into the mud to slow his descent.

Seconds later he shouted up to us, "All clear!"

"Mole, you next." I grabbed the ruck from his hand. "Go!"

He turned and dropped into a seated position. Holding the CAR-15 across his chest, he slid down into the dark mouth of the garbage dump, shouting, "Ohhh, shit!"

Cassidy fastened two ropes to the end of the poncho near Zak's feet. Zak held onto the cords extending upward over his chest as we lowered him down the chute. Heavy fire still droned from the west.

"Lee-lin, go!" I said, pulling the claymores and the time pencils from the ruck.

Cassidy knelt near me as I began carefully inserting blasting caps into an arming well. "What are those?"

"Never mind. Get over to the west side and pull that fire team back here. They should have been here by now."

"Here they come," Cino said, looking up at two Marines running toward us.

"They're on us, Sarge!" a man yelled while clutching his hand.

"Where's Clint, Dobbins, Taylor?" Cino shouted.

"Dead! They're dead!"

I jerked a nod toward the wall. "Over the wall. You too, Tonto!"

I quickly primed each claymore and positioned them several feet apart, aiming them inward toward the hill crest. I pulled the fuse igniters, then grabbed the AK and crawled to the exit hole.

I'd cut the time fuse for a four-minute delay. I knew the three claymores I'd put out would only put a dent in the mass of Communists overrunning us, but hopefully, the mines would give us a little extra escape time.

Glancing back over my shoulder, I slid down the muddy trough, whispering, "*Sat-cong*, motherfuckers, *sat-cong*."

Chapter 25

With maximized noise discipline we slipped out of the muddy stink of the garbage dump and into the pitch-black jungle. If I'd counted right, I had six men, plus Zak and Lee-lin, with me.

Cassidy took point and led us into a thicket. Then he and two Marines moved into a security position at the edge of the thicket while I administered the last Syrette of morphine to the gunny.

The distant thunder of my claymore detonations brought Zak's head forward. "What's that?"

"A little surprise I left for Chuck. How you holding up?"

"Better, now that I got that morphine. I thought you said—"

I looked at Lee-lin. "You stay here with Zak. I'm going to find Shilo and get his arm wrapped."

I crawled, weaving my way through the wet bamboo darkness, whispering Shilo's name.

Mole's faint voice floated through the night. "Brett—Brett. Over here."

I found Mole cradling Shilo's head in his lap. "He's sleeping, Brett. He's—he's lost a lot of blood. I think—

think he was shot in the stomach. I—I can feel blood down—''

"Negative, he took a round in the arm," I said, feeling the wet texture of the cravat around Shilo's arm. His skin was cool to the touch. I quickly felt for a pulse beneath his armpit. My fingers sensed a faint beat.

I tapped his face lightly, "Shilo, wake up. It's Yancy. Wake up, partner."

No response.

"Brett, I'm sure—sure, there's a lot of blood down here."

I ran my fingers beneath Shilo's shirt. Probing the blood-soaked contour of his stomach, I found a finger-sized hole in his side.

"Shit. He's been gut shot too. Give me your cravat, Mole."

I folded the cloth, placed it over the wound, and took Mole's hand and placed it on the cloth. "Hold this . . . keep a firm pressure on it."

My fingers groped frantically through my aid pouch, searching for an amyl-nitrate capsule. Shilo was in shock—I had to stop the bleeding and get him awake fast.

I grasped the small gauze-wrapped capsule, cracked it open, and jammed it beneath his nostrils. "Shilo, it's Yancy! You gotta wake up, partner. It's Yancy. Wake the fuck up!" I whispered emphatically.

His head jerked slightly away from the strong nitrate stink.

I kept the capsule poised at his nose. "That's it, buddy, breathe this shit. Breathe. Why didn't you tell me you'd been gut shot?"

Mole whispered, "Brett, he feels real cold."

Finally, Shilo muttered weakly, "Didn't . . . want to slow down the . . . march." He tried to raise his head.

"Stay calm, partner. Stay calm. You're gonna make it."

He coughed. "I—I can hear—'Gary Owen'—buddy. I think Custer's callin' me in. I ain't gonna make it, Brett."

"Yes, you are, goddammit! You're gonna make it!"

He whispered, "Brett, come, come closer. I gotta ask you something."

I leaned down to his dark face. "What is it, partner?"

He cracked a half grin. "Hey, partner, don't you think . . . think . . . Custer would have . . . been proud of us tonight?"

I mashed the nitrate capsule into the wet earth, then caressed his nape. "Roger. Damn proud," I whispered, searching my mind for words to console the dying warrior.

"Shilo, do you remember in that Custer movie, when he comes face-to-face with Striker, across the bar?"

"Yeah . . . yeah," he said, trying to smile.

"And when Striker told Custer that money was better than glory, Custer looked back at him with cold steel eyes and said, 'Maybe, Striker, but there's one thing to be said for glory: When it comes your time to go, you can take glory with you!' Remember?"

"Yeah . . . I remember that," he mumbled.

The warrior Shilo smiled. His eyelids closed slowly— his smile didn't fade.

I gently raised Shilo's limp body away from Mole and pulled the ammo belt away from his shoulders.

Mole sniffed and wiped at his eyes. "Brett, I'd like to say—say a prayer for him."

Cassidy's urgent voice intruded as he crawled toward

me. "We got trackers on us! We gotta move now." He glanced at Mole kneeling over Shilo. "Is he dead?"

"Yes! How many trackers?" I asked quickly.

"Don't know. Maybe six."

My first instinct was to lay a hasty ambush and nail the bastards. But with Zak and Lee-lin to consider, I decided to move. I'd try to raise Moonbeam on the radio after we shook the trackers.

"Okay, Cino, take us due east a hundred meters, then hook south toward Khe Sanh. And don't lose that radio."

Forty minutes later first light began to caress the morning. With the cloak of darkness lifting its veil and no rain, Chuck would probably be making some good time tracking us. Right now, the only thing we had going for us was ground fog—it would be fading soon. Our movement had been slow and arduous. On one occasion they dropped Zak, but he didn't yell out.

Looking ahead, I saw Cassidy hurrying back toward me. He stopped short when he saw Shilo draped over my shoulder. "Have you been carrying him all this way?"

"Roger. What's our proximity?"

"Near the burned chopper."

I eased Shilo's body down and motioned to the men carrying Zak to lower him to the ground.

The gunny woke abruptly. "Where are we?"

I knelt next to him. "We're heading toward Khe Sanh. You doing okay?"

"I had better days in boot camp," he said.

I turned to Cassidy. "Give me that radio. I'm going to try and get Moonbeam on the horn. How about you making a little retro-recon on those trackers?"

Cassidy looked around, studying the trees as he removed the radio backpack. "Brett, I'm gettin' that feeling again."

I glanced up at him. "Don't tell me that, Tonto. I need some good news right now!" For once, I was hoping that Cino's sixth sense needed calibration.

I flipped the radio to the guard frequency. Cassidy moved out in the direction we'd just traversed.

Moments later I still hadn't been able to raise Moonbeam on either the primary or alternate freq. Lee-lin moved near me and squatted. "Yon-cee," she whispered. "You saying need good new. Maybe, I'm having good new."

"Lee-lin, I don't need any bullshit right now, so . . ." I stopped, realizing my voice was tired. I looked over at her. "Okay, darlin', what's on your mind?"

"I'm know dis place here good." She pointed in a half circle as she spoke. "VC have tail near dat way." She motioned east.

"Tail? You mean trail, right?"

"Yes, dat what I'm say, tail. Tail having some . . ." She paused as if trying to think of a word. "Tail having some booby tak, but I'm knowing where is." She smiled.

I moved closer to her. "Okay, Lee-lin, the tail—trail—has booby traps, and you can lead us around them. But where does trail go?"

"It go to big open place. Good new for heli-chop. Yes?"

I wasn't quite as elated about Lee-lin's good-news revelation as she seemed to be. Although she'd thoughtfully called my attention to a potential exfil LZ, that wasn't much benefit to us without a chopper. Nonetheless, I pulled the map out of my pocket and tried to find the location she was talking about.

There was only one open area depicted that was anywhere near the Enola Hetero crash site. It was close, approximately eighty meters due east. I had to admit that it was a lot closer than Khe Sanh, considering the loads we were carrying.

The fact that we could use a trail made the idea even more appealing. Ordinarily, I'd be skeptical of ambushes on a trail. But I knew damn well that the massive siege on Hill 950 had required every soldier and ablebodied conscript they had in the area to join the assault. With the exception of the trackers, the chances were good that this area was clear of enemy.

I checked my watch: 0550 hours. Moonbeam would be replaced by Sunburst shortly. I'd wait and try my luck with Sunburst, then I'd decide which way to go.

I looked at Lee-lin. "Darlin', your tail may be very good." I blinked, thinking about what I'd just said. I decided not to try and correct it.

Chapter 26

Mole Mackenzie leaned against a tree in the dim morning light, trying to stay awake. His head tilted slowly downward, then rose abruptly when his chin touched the upper edge of his poncho. Everyone was tired—everyone but Cassidy.

It was now 0610 hours and I still hadn't been able to raise Sunburst. Strong breezes stirred the foliage as Cino crept back into our position.

"Can't find no trackers."

"Well, that's a hint of good news," I replied.

"No it ain't. It bugs me when I don't know where they are."

I poked my finger at the clearing on the map. "I'm not going to argue with you; look at this. There's a suitable LZ due east of here. Do you know where it—"

"Yep. Eighty meters that way." He nodded east.

I looked around, noticing the advance of morning light, then turned to Cino. "I want you to take Lee-lin on point with you and get us on the trail. She knows where all the booby traps are located. Let's move."

I knew the decision to move east all but snuffed my original plans to conduct a rock quarry recon, but the situation had changed dramatically. Right now my priority was to get us out of the mouth of the tiger.

Standing, I looked at Lee-lin. She was holding the pistol by the barrel. I took the weapon from her, turned it around, and placed the butt back into her palm. "There, it works better that way, darlin'. Now, I want you to go with Cassidy and show him where the booby traps are, okay?"

"Rog-ee, Yon-cee."

Mole and the three other Marines had stationed themselves, one at each corner of the poncho. As they lifted Zak, I lowered the radio onto the poncho next to him. I placed the handset in his grip, then positioned the whip antenna vertically.

"Zak, if you can, try and give Sunburst a call every now and then while we're moving. Okay?"

"Roger. Let's press on." His voice was lethargic.

I turned and lifted Shilo's body up and over my shoulder.

When we got on the trail it felt like a super-highway compared to the trip, stumble, and fall route we'd just come out of. We skirted around three booby traps during the movement to LZ Lee-lin. Two of the traps Lee-lin pointed out were set with low trip wires running back to M-26 grenades. The other was a wide, well-concealed *punji* pit.

I decided not to disarm the grenades so as not to reveal our presence and direction of movement if Chuck came wandering back this way.

As we approached the edge of the LZ, my eyes looked eagerly upward. Puff-topped cumulus clouds blotched the sky. The bases were above two thousand feet. Morning sun cracked through wide breaks in the cloud cover as a brisk wind raked over the five-foot elephant grass spanning the open field. The air smelled clean.

The trail we came in on continued straight ahead, cutting through the center of the swaying grass. I could see that it narrowed into a smaller path a few meters into the grass.

We moved into the left-side treeline. Cassidy helped me ease Shilo off my shoulders and down. I stood and raised my hand to shade my eyes and took a slow look around the entire circumference of the LZ.

Lee-lin quietly informed me that the trail dissecting the center of the field was clear of booby traps—but my concern right now was potential observation by an LZ sitter.

Cassidy squatted near Shilo's body while Mole and the other Marines moved Zak near me.

"Brett, I didn't hear a peep outa anybody," Zak's tired voice whispered.

I glanced back into the forest, then down at the gunny. "I'm not surprised, Zak. That triple canopy is hard to get a signal through, sometimes. And that battery is probably weak by now," I said, picking the radio up. "We should have better luck out here in the open."

I looked at Cino. "How about you doing your best sneak-and-peek routine around the LZ while I try to raise Sunburst. Check these trees for LZ sitters."

He grinned as if I was making a joke. "LZ sitters! Are you shittin'—kidding me?"

I knew Cassidy hadn't had much experience with air operations—but I had. I explained to him that frequently Chuck would station a man up in a tree with the sole purpose in life of watching a potential landing zone. If he spotted an incoming chopper or personnel on the LZ, he would then fire a series of rifle code shots to alert the local reaction force. The practice was common in Laos where they often used lame or injured soldiers as observers.

I wasn't certain they used the same tactic in this area, but it was possible. We'd just come out of a nightmare on Zulu—there was no sense in letting our guard down now that we were near an exit.

After Cino left I knelt by the radio. As I called Sunburst I noticed Mole pull a canteen out and pass it down to Zak.

"Sunburst, this is Mayday Zulu. Over. Sunburst, this is Mayday Zulu. Over."

"Mayday Zulu, this is Sunburst. Loud and clear. Over."

My pulse quickened. I tried not to hurry my words. "Roger, Sunburst, same-same. Message follows. Hill Niner-five-zero has been overrun. I say again overrun. I have eight personnel that made it out. Require exfil immediately. I say again, require immediate exfil of eight personnel ASAP. Over."

"Roger, Zulu. Copy, exfil eight personnel. Be advised, Foxtrot-Alpha-Charlie has launched from Phu Bai to check that area. Zulu missed six commo checks last night. We figured something was up, but could not get an aircraft in to that area. Can you give me a grid on your location? Over."

I couldn't take the chance on transmitting our position in the clear. I glanced upward. The clouds were still allowing streaks of sun to stab through.

I keyed again. "Sunburst, Zulu. Negative on grid. Cannot transmit in clear. Advise Foxtrot-Alpha-Charlie that I will use a shiny when he gets in the area. Over."

"Roger, Zulu. Understand shiny. I'm working another ball game right now. I will contact Foxtrot-Alpha-Charlie and tell him to look for shiny. Stay on this push.

His call sign is Ghost Rider. He should be on station in about three-zero. After he pulls you, he'll be working a body recovery on that downed chopper. Over."

I glanced at my watch: 0620. "Roger, Sunburst. Copy. Thanks a bunch. I owe you bowl of Texas chili. Zulu out."

"Roger, Texas chili. Sunburst out."

Everyone's eyes searched the sky. It was now 0635 hours. Cassidy had not returned to our position. I darted glances between the sky, my watch, and the trail leading back into the jungle. Every minute we stayed here the more time Chuck had to find us.

I had positioned two of the Marines, Kincaid and Eagleston, as linear security listening posts. After another moment of waiting I decided to go out and check with them to see if they had seen or heard from Cassidy.

"Mole," I whispered. "Come here, amigo."

Lee-lin accompanied Mole, carrying the pistol in one hand and Mole's canteen in the other. As he hurried toward me he stumbled. I reached out and grabbed his arm to keep him from falling.

"Sorry, Brett. I'm—I'm kinda—"

"That's all right, partner. We're all a little tired. I want you to monitor this radio while I go check for Cino. If you see an OV-2, a FAC, I want you to contact him. His call sign is Ghost Rider. Roger?"

"His call sign is Ghost Rider Roger?" Mole muttered.

"No, Mackenzie. Just Ghost Rider. We're Zulu. Got it?"

"Yes, I—I got it."

I winked at Lee-lin. "Don't let him fall asleep. Watch sky."

I checked with Kincaid, who reported he hadn't seen

a sign of Cassidy or Chuck. The only thing Eagleston had observed was a deer.

As I crept away from Eagleston's position I heard a muffled burst of M16 fire coming from the direction of the trail. I dug a crusted wad of blood from my ear and listened closer. Another burst resounded in the distance.

"No AK fire," I whispered to myself. It sounded like a short, one-sided firefight—an ambush.

I glanced back at Eagleston. "You stay here. I'll check it out."

I hurried into the damp shadows of the jungle. After a moment my eyes began to adjust to the dim light. My tired senses were suddenly alerted to the noise of my body brushing against the drooping vines and my quick steps crushing into the wet undergrowth. I was moving too fast. I slowed, keeping the muzzle of my AK leveled in my direction of travel.

I moved near the trail and paralleled it, staying a few feet away from it. A few cautious steps farther I saw a bend in the trail just beyond the *punji* pit area that Lee-lin had pointed out earlier.

As I eased around the bend I saw the dim silhouette of someone hunkered over a body in the center of the trail. My finger slowly took in the trigger slack.

Moving silently closer, I heard a low-toned voice. "And now, one for you. Open wide, Anus."

It was Cassidy. He was leaning over a dead pajama-clad VC body sprawled face-up in the thin veil of fog. I could see that the body was missing the left arm. It appeared to have been amputated below the elbow.

I squinted, seeing something that looked like a short, blackened piece of time fuse protruding out of the VC's mouth. Next to this body was another one. There were no visible signs of weapons, but there were two small rucksacks lying near the bodies. The rucks appeared to be the type issued by the South Vietnamese Army.

Moving forward, I decided to use a verbal alert rather than risk surprising him with any noise I might make coming out of the bush.

"Dallas Cowboys!" I whispered loudly.

Cassidy whirled, jerking his rifle toward me.

"Hold it! It's me, Yancy," I said, stepping out from beneath the limbs. Cino jumped to his feet as I came closer.

He spoke while moving to block my view. "I greased our trackers. We don't have to worry about these anuses anymore."

I looked at his frowning eyes, then stepped around him and looked at the bodies. They'd been chest shot. He'd rolled them over onto their backs. A long rat tail jutted from each man's gaping mouth. The black tails hanging from their mouths gave them the appearance of human lizards.

I lowered my AK and looked over at Cassidy. "What the fuck is with the rat tails? Is this your idea of a calling card?"

He smirked, looking down at the skinny bodies. "Yeah, you might say that. Lets their buddies know I been here," he said proudly. He shrugged. "So what? I didn't take their ears!"

Looking back down at the bloody bodies, I noticed that both men were arm amputees.

Cassidy turned. "I'll just throw these rucks back off the trail."

"Hold it, Cino!" I said, moving in front of him. "These aren't trackers. They don't even have weapons. They're VC all right, but they're not soldiers anymore. Probably lost their limbs in some battle.

"Now they're working as couriers. They run intel up north and return with anything from a few rocket rounds to messages from Giap's headquarters."

I glanced at Cassidy's poker face, aware that I wasn't telling him anything he didn't already know. I knelt near a ruck and began loosening the straps. "Let's see what they're hauling today."

I'd seen VC couriers before. Will and I had nailed two of them during a mission into Laos. They always traveled in pairs so that in case one of them got snakebit or injured in some way, the other could treat him. They moved fast. SOG headquarters estimated that the NVA had hundreds of the VC "backpackers" running constantly back and forth from north to south like relentless streams of ants. They were General Giap's human communication and ammo resupply chain.

In South Vietnam, when a soldier lost an arm or leg he was banished to the market to beg. In Uncle Ho's army they went to work as couriers or LZ sitters.

But neither one of them gave a damn about their disabled vets.

Chapter 27

As my fingers worked the straps loose from the small retainer clips on the rucksack, it suddenly dawned on me why Cassidy was a big name on the NVA most wanted list. He'd evidently been interdicting the local "backpack" teams for some time now during his solo excursions.

At some point in time he'd probably been spied stuffing one of his business cards in a victim's mouth, and he was easily identifiable by his rat-tail necklace—either that or his odor.

I didn't know why Cino was playing dumb about the couriers, but at any rate, he was putting a big gash in one of Giap's primary arteries and it was obvious Chuck didn't like it one bit.

I'd already guessed that Cassidy might be taking gold out of the quarry, so if that was true, it appeared that the combined impact of Cino's gold pilfering and courier ambushes was tearing Chuck a new asshole in this area. Cassidy wasn't necessarily a one-man army, but he did qualify as a Gatling gun in a pistol match.

I opened the flap on the rucksack, pulled the inside drawstring loose, and took out a large bag of rice. Underneath a bottle of water I found a canvas case full of documents written in Vietnamese. Flipping through them I found drawings of several military fortifications, a *chu-hoi* pass issued by the South Vietnamese government, and some black-and-white photos of an American airfield.

I glanced at my watch. I still had ten minutes before Ghost Rider was due onstation.

I placed the photos aside. "Tonto, I'm probably not telling you something you don't already know, but you've just prevented one more package of intel from—" I stopped in midsentence as I felt the velvety texture of a small bag in the bottom of the rucksack.

Pulling it from the ruck, I immediately saw the familiar yellow Crown Royal symbol on the dirty blue pouch. "This Cong has expensive taste," I said, yanking the drawstrings loose on the small bag.

Cassidy squatted beside me like a silent Montagnard as I dug my hand into the bag and withdrew an assortment of rings, pendants, and gold chains. He reached into my palm and picked out what looked like a class ring.

Examining it he said, "Wow, this *lo-dit* graduated from the United States Air Force Academy, class of '63!"

I ignored Cino's wit and dug deeper into the bag. I removed a Rolex Submariner watch and a small wad of greenbacks held by a rubber band. I carefully poured the jewelry back into the small bag, then quickly counted through the assortment of ten-, twenty-, and hundred-dollar bills.

"Eight hundred and sixty dollars!" I said, looking at Cino. "Not to mention what all this other loot is worth."

Cassidy smiled proudly, then looked upward and frowned. "I hear something, Brett."

Looking up, I heard the drone of a small plane.

"That's got to be our FAC, partner." I thrust the bills into the pouch and pulled the strings closed.

I stood. "Grab that other ruck. We need to get back to the LZ," I said, pushing the Crown Royal bag into my side pants pocket.

Grabbing my AK, I turned and hurried down the trail. "Let's go, Tonto."

As I approached the open area I saw the outline of an OV-2 banking northward between breaks in the clouds. Sunlight stabbed my eyes.

I jerked my aid pouch open and removed a small, stainless-steel signal mirror. Tilting the mirror I picked up the glare of the sun and walked the reflection carefully toward the near side of the banking aircraft.

Mole ran to me carrying the radio. "Here, Brett. Here's the—the . . . Do you think that's Ghost Rider?"

I moved my hand, keeping the small patch of reflected sunlight fixed on the aircraft as it arched through the sky. "Give me the handset, Mole," I said, keeping my eyes concentrated skyward.

Mole held the radio while I keyed the handset. "Ghost Rider, this is Zulu. Do you have my shiny? Over."

I could hear the background purr of the engine as he answered. "Zulu, this is Ghost Rider. Roger your shiny. You look like a Cadillac hubcap down there, amigo. Are you in contact? Over."

"This is Zulu. Negative contact. But we've got Charlie in the area. Over."

"Roger, Zulu. Understand, Charlie in the woods. I got two foxtrot-fours and a slick peddlin' this way. They're about ten minutes out. I'm scoping Hill Nine-fifty right now. Can't see nothing but smoke over there. Charlie musta moved out. Over."

"Roger copy, Ghost Rider. If those foxtrot-fours have

nape on board, how about having them lay a few pods five-zero meters off the west side of my location. Over?"

"Copy, Zulu. You want a napalm bonfire five-zero meters west of your location. Can do. Stand by."

"Zulu standing by. Out."

It didn't surprise me that Chuck had exited Hill 950. He knew the clearing weather would allow tac-air to get in and pulverize him if he hung around long. I'd requested the napalm run to put a flaming buffer between LZ Lee-lin and any NVA that might be moving in on us from the west.

I gave the handset back to Mole and looked around for Tonto. "Mole, have you seen Cassidy?"

"No, but we heard fire coming from down the trail a while ago."

"Roger. I know about that, but I thought Cino was right behind me coming out of there."

I looked back toward the trail. "You stay on that radio. I'm going to look for Cino. If I'm not back in ten minutes, tell Ghost Rider to hold off on that napalm run."

A few meters down the trail I saw Cassidy squatting off to one side of the path. At first I thought he was "passing stool," but looking closer I could see that he was writing something on a small piece of paper.

As I approached he folded the paper into a square. "What are you doing, Tonto?" I said, looking down at him.

He didn't stand. "Just writin' a note," he mumbled without looking up at me.

He removed a small, tattered American flag from his shirt pocket, carefully folded it around the note, and handed it up to me. "Why don't you hang on to this?"

I reached out and took the flag-wrapped note. "What's this?"

"It's the last official act of Kirk Henderson. He was killed takin' that off the commo bunker antenna. You see, Marines got this thing about the flag." He glanced at my hands. "That little faded piece of cloth don't mean much to some people at home, but to a Marine, it's top of the page. Anyhow, thought you might make sure it gets home to Kirk's folks. He'd like that."

"Sure, I'll do that. But we're getting out of here in about twenty minutes. Why don't you take it and—"

"Ain't going, Brett!"

I stepped closer. "Now wait a minute, Cassidy. What did—"

"You heard me. I'm stayin'." He rose slowly and leveled a stare at me.

I frowned. "You don't seem to understand something, Tonto. You don't have any fucking place to stay! Zulu is over, partner. They may never put an outpost up there again. What are you going to eat out here? Never mind, stupid question."

He grinned. "It was good soldiering with you, Yancy. You really should have been a Marine." He turned to walk away. "I gotta go."

I jumped forward into the bush and grabbed his shoulder, turning him face-to-face with me. "Okay, Cassidy, stay here and play your fucking game with Charlie! You like this shit!

"But before you just slide away into the sunrise, I got a question for you."

"Make it quick, Brett. I'm double parked." He smirked as if he enjoyed seeing me pissed-off. I thought about knocking him out and taking him with me like it or not. As quickly as the thought came to me he seemed to read my eyes and stepped out of fist range. "What? What's your question, Yancy?"

"All right, all right. You and Jake Ray have been hauling gold out of a mine in the quarry, right or wrong?"

He laughed. "Gold mine? Have you been smokin' those left-wing Luckies? There ain't no gold mine up here."

"Don't bullshit me, Cassidy! I lifted Ray's ruck back in that bunker at Khe Sanh. It felt like a ton of lead. You're getting rich up here. That's why you want to stay here!"

Cassidy lowered his head slowly. He spoke without looking up. "You're dead wrong about that. Money don't mean much to me, 'cept for what it can do for my friends."

He raised his head and cracked a half grin. "Yeah, but you are right about one thing. Jake's ruck was full of the same shit we took off the packers. Jake's got over forty-three thousand dollars in green and about sixty pounds of rings, watches, gold chains . . . same type stuff you got in your pocket there. Jake and I figure the stuff is worth another forty thousand, easy.

"That totals around eighty thousand, and you know where it's all goin', Yancy? After Jake sells the jewelry it's all going to Mole's family to help his sister. That's where it's going."

I glanced down at the ground fog hovering around my feet, then looked up and smiled at the dirtiest man I'd ever seen. "Cassidy, you damn near qualify as noble. That's great what you and Jake are doing for Mole. Sorry I—"

"Don't apologize. But I'd just as soon Mole didn't